BENEATH THE WATER'S EDGE

A Romancing the Pirate Novella

Jennifer Bray-Weber

Copyright © 2012 Jennifer Bray-Weber

All rights reserved.

ISBN-13: 978-1469957142
ISBN-10: 1469957140

Acknowledgements

A heartfelt thank you to my friends and writing buddies for your generous championing and encouragement you've lavished upon me every step of the way.

A special thank you to Rhonda Morrow, Kim Killion, Stacey Purcell, and Eliza Knight for the invaluable support in this book's finishing touches.

Of course, I would be nowhere without the continued love and support from my family. Thank you for believing in me always.

CHAPTER 1

Caribbean Sea, due north of Anguilla, 1719

"On your feet, boy! Fight like a man."
Boy? Elyssa Calhoun Montgomery scampered on her bottom away from the boorish pirate. Pain shot through her jaw from the hit she took from the invader. Blood, metallic and tart, filled her mouth. She shook away the white dots blurring her vision and flattened her back against the mast. *He mustn't know the truth.*
Pirates had boarded the Spanish merchant ship *Maravilla* when her captain failed to outrun their sloop. Steel striking steel, gunfire, and vagrant shouts crowded her ears. Sweat and gun smoke clogged her nose. Chaos poured across the decks. Battles all around her were fought in pairs. Now Elyssa was forced to fight like a real man for her life, or lose it. Only she had no weapon. Nor had she ever hit anyone before. Nor was she a man.
She scooted backward up the pole, her wobbly knees hardly holding her upright.
"Come on, ya little whelp." The pirate's sneer spread into a toothless grin. "'Fore I gut ya." He pulled a gulley knife from the tattered green sash around his waist. Despite

the rough-hewn handle, the blade glimmered, well-cleaned and sharpened, in the sunlight. Elyssa swallowed the lump lodged in her throat and tampered down the fear burgeoning her insides. No time for vapors like some mollycoddled gentry, not if she were to survive. On a barrel beside her lay the marlinespike she'd been using to separate the cords of a damaged rope when the pirates appeared. It wasn't as impressive as the man's knife, but with its long metal pick, it would have to do. She snatched it up and held it out in front of her.

"Stay back," she warned. "Or I'll plug you between the eyes." She waved the spike making sure the man knew she meant business.

"Blimey." The pirate chuckled. "This 'ere's a waste o' good fightin'. I needs ta find me a tar who ain't so lily-livered."

Never had Elyssa seen a man move so fast. He grabbed her wrist and twisted, slamming her against the mast. She yelped at the sharp smarting. Dropping her weapon, the marlinspike clattered to the floor. His retched breath fell upon her face. "Death is but yer due, boy." The tip of the blade of his knife pricked her throat's tender flesh. "Unless ye be joinin' the ranks of the devil."

Dear Lord, pressed into the service of a pirate crew or die. What choice did she have?

The *Maravilla* was weeks out from sailing into San Juan. Elyssa was a mere fortnight away from no longer pretending to be a young man working as a deckhand. A fortnight away from freedom. Now, it was gone. Her freedom gone. Again.

This couldn't be happening.

"Well, boy? Whassit gonna be?"

Elyssa's heart raced, she couldn't quite catch her breath as he crushed his slovenly body harder against her. Tears borne of sheer terror threatened and she bit her bottom lip in a desperate bid to control its quivering.

The severe stitch in the pirate's brow loosened. Confusion first, then recognition of something amiss flickered in his black eyes. Did he know? Had he figured out she was not as she seemed? He swept her features, no doubt looking from some clue.

How long could she keep up her disguise? Surely she would meet an unsavory fate among pirates should her ruse be discovered. But torture and dying wasn't an option. She'd made it this far without incident. Aye, she'd continue this hoax as long as she could, and at first chance, she'd flee. She had dreams to build.

Elyssa nodded once, not lending her voice to his suspicion. The pirate tilted his head, staring hard. Long moments passed. Her heartbeat thumped louder in her as ears as the sounds of fighting died. She was certain she would buckle under his intense scrutiny.

"Huzzah, men!"

Elyssa didn't dare unlock eyes with the wretch to find the source of the deep, rich voice.

"The Spanish bastards have surrendered. We've taken ourselves a mighty fine prize. Round 'em up!" Cheers erupted, pistols raised, pops fired in celebration.

Pirates herded the *Maravilla* jack-tars to the center of the ship.

The man pinning Elyssa finally stepped away. He glanced around before his eyes landed upon her again. "Join the others, *lad*."

She didn't like his tone, not at all. And with the quick curl of his lip, she reckoned he had her figured out.

Helpless to do little more to improve her situation, Elyssa followed orders and stood among her fellow crewmen. The battle had lasted a handful of minutes. Tangy scents of blood ousted the smoke wafting away on the breezes. Slick red stains soaked through several of *Maravilla's* men, but none suffered more than flesh wounds. Elyssa breathed easier knowing all had survived the attack. It had become necessary to avoid friendships with the men she had worked alongside for the past month. Still, she wouldn't want anyone killed.

"All right, all right. Hold your gab." A smartly dressed pirate in a fine dark blue vest and black breeches climbed two steps up the quarterdeck ladder. Short blond locks flipped out under the faded yellow scarf wrapped tightly around his head. He flicked his arm up for everyone's attention. "Capt'n Blackthorn speaks."

"Obliged, Mister Kipp."

Elyssa recognized the deep voice as the one who earlier claimed victory. He stepped to the deck railing and her breath hitched.

Perhaps it was his vantage overlooking the flock of them. Perhaps it was how he held his back straight with intense confidence. Whatever the case, the pirate captain seemed impossibly tall. He wore a long black dress coat with shiny brass buttons and clean knee breeches fastened with crimson garters. Indubitably, the rogue could pass for a king. He was trimmed in impeccable finery, from his buckled shoes to his ringed fingers. Despite his gentlemanly fashion, there was no mistaking the impressive bandolier of pistols strapped to his chest. He was a dangerous man, to be sure. She couldn't make out his features clearly under the shadows of his red plumed hat, but his slow, shrewd scan of the crowd sent shivers across her skin.

"A fair afternoon to you, men. I am called Captain Bran Blackthorn of the *Sanctum*. Welcome to my waters upon which you trespass." He threw his arms wide, gesturing the ocean near and far belonged solely to him. "Now with pleasantries out of the way, I will speak of the business at hand."

He waved to men behind him. "Your captain, Alonso, is it?" The pirates brought *Maravilla's* captain forward. Like the defeat hung from his frown, shackles hung from his wrists. Elyssa thought Captain Alonso to be an arrogant man.

But now 'twas obvious he had been knocked from his grand horse and humbled.

"Aye, Alonso," Captain Blackthorn said. "Alonso kindly relinquished his cargo of goods. A fair trade for his life, I think. Most especially after engaging me with his pathetic hand piece." The pirate captain let a small gun hang from his finger. "My men will also seize anything they deem valuable for our trouble, including your weapons, clothing, and tools." He tossed the pistol to Mister Kipp. "'Tis nothing personal, mind you." He tipped his head as if it was an unavoidable fact.

"Accordingly, let me lay forth your fates. I am a just man. Am I not, Mister Kipp?"

Mister Kipp, leaning against the ladder, spun a gulley knife in and around the fingers of one hand. The speed and dexterity of his talent impressed Elyssa. More so than his alarmingly relaxed confidence. She wondered how he didn't slice a digit clean off.

"Aye," he said. "No better a just man there was, Capt'n."

"Yes, yes. You're right of course, Mister Kipp," he said, nodding. "I believe in choices. And I shall offer one to you. Join my band of merry buccaneers. Adventure, coin, and a taste of wanton women can be yours."

The pirates chuckled, as though no better life could be had.

"Be apprised," Captain Blackthorn continued. "'Tis grueling work. And you will be an enemy to every country, hunted down and quite possibly hanged from a hempen necklace. Or, should this sound unsavory, then you shall chance the sea with your captain."

He cast his judgment toward the defeated captain, shaking his head in disappointment. "Captain Alonso's unfortunate mistake cost him. As a consequence, those of you loyal to your leader will do so with the provisions of one day."

"One day?"

The lad beside Elyssa should have kept quiet, but he continued to wag his unwise tongue.

"We'll starve!"

He immediately met with a punch to his gut by the nearest pirate. Elyssa cringed. The poor fellow buckled, spitting, gasping for air.

Captain Blackthorn descended the ladder and crouched down in front of the unfortunate man. "Boy, you know nothing of starvation. Nothing," he growled. He stood and his height matched his formidable authority. With biting sarcasm, he added, "Let us hope the winds deliver you to a safe port and you do not suffer too terribly from your hunger."

With keen eyes, he scanned the crowd. He radiated malice. But Elyssa found herself more curious than scared. She fixated on those eyes, eyes not as brown as his long hair tied at the nape of his neck. Their unusual light color contrasted with his swarthy skin. How could a man, indeed a villainous pirate, have such beautiful eyes?

"Those of you wishing to go on account step forward," Captain Blackthorn said.

Glances to one another, marked by indecision, flitted through the *Maravilla* men. One by one, men moved out of the crowd to join Captain Blackthorn's crew.

She searched for the pirate who threatened her. The wretch leaned against the mast, cleaning his fingernails with his gulley knife. He pinned her with an expectant stare. She gulped down the sickened taste building in her mouth. No doubt should she refuse, she'd be exposed on the spot for the sham she was, or worse, dead before the last chest of slops exchanged ships. Elyssa took the step forward, knowing her life may change forever.

Captain Blackthorn measured up those who chose to join the *Sanctum*. What a sorry excuse for seamen. Green and desperate, not fit for a jollyboat. Blackthorn's own ragtag and bobtail men fared in better shape than these labbernecks.

"Only twelve…" His gaze landed upon a young lad to his left. What a pitiful looking choir boy. Probably cried for his mama when he received that split lip. Blimey. The beanrake hardly reached his chest. Small shoulders, tiny hands, probably couldn't lift more than a bucket of water. Perhaps those spindly arms offer him advantages climbing the rigging.

"Make that twelve and a half, brave souls, eh? So be it. Welcome to the brotherhood, lads."

Blackthorn couldn't afford to be particular. He'd lost several fine men to sickness and several more in battle. He needed as many men as willing to sign the *Sanctum's* articles.

He spun on his heel, strode to the side of the ship, and jumped to the gunwale. Hanging onto a line, he turned around, flashing a smirk. "Tonight, we celebrate our latest victory."

A roar of joy erupted from the pirate crew. Talk of rum and music added to the good cheer. This night his men would have full bellies, as well. 'Twas good fortune to cross courses with the Spanish vessel. Rations were running dangerously low and Blackthorn didn't expect to meet up with Christensen for another month. Maybe two. When Christensen did find him, Blackthorn hoped his old friend came bearing good news, not open gun ports.

Kipp addressed the newest recruits. "Honeymoon's over, boys. Go below and help fetch up the cargo. The rest of you set yourself down. They'll be no need of yer sorry arses. And doncha even think of doin' somethin' foolish, lest ye be thrown to the sharks."

Blackthorn stepped over to the *Sanctum's* gunwale and hopped down, his coat billowing behind him. He stopped before the hatch leading to his quarters and looked back. The young boy stared at him as if were the King of Spain.

Blackthorn chuckled. Poor runt. In awe of a pauper instead of a prince. But then Blackthorn could very well call himself royalty. He ruled this part of the Caribbean. 'Twas all a matter of perception.

Kipp snapped his fingers in front of the lad's face. "You there."

The boy flinched.

"Ya got barnacles in yer lugholes? Get below." Kipp gave him a swift kick in the rear as the lad hurried past, joining the others in plunder.

That boy's going to need breaking.

Elyssa rested atop *Sanctum's* skylight. The sails above pocketed the winds and the ship sliced through the glassy sapphire sea. Blustery breezes caressed her cheeks and cooled her damp skin. She was glad for the spot of respite. Her arms burned and back ached. Lugging crates and rolling barrels from boat to boat took a toll on her. She couldn't remember a time she had worked so hard, not in all her life. Since Dobie had dressed her up as a boy, passing her along as his younger brother, and signing them both up for the *Maravilla* crew, she had become stronger than she could imagine. No longer a waif, fragile girl. Ironic that she would survive and Dobie would perish under the harsh conditions as a deck hand.

The *Maravilla* lingered on the horizon much like a stunned, wounded animal. She wondered what would be the fate of Captain Alonso and his men. Surely they would make it to some port nearby. After all, the pirates left him with his sails. How odd that they did. All the tales she'd ever heard were of marauders taking all and leaving nothing, sinking ships or setting them ablaze. 'Twas as if Captain Blackthorn gave the *Maravilla* a fighting chance.

Elyssa listened to the flurry of whispers from her fellow crewmen.

"I think we be lucky, mates."

"I heard the *Sanctum* has captured Spanish galleons laden with silver."

"And I heard Capt'n Blackthorn cheated the devil from claiming his soul."

"Aye. I'll take my chances with a capt'n like that."

"Or die alongside 'im."

"'Twould be worth it, I say, with pockets full o' coin, drunk, and buried within a pretty wench."

The men prattled on of riches, adventure, and women. But Elyssa focused on the distant sun settling into a sparkling ocean blanket, patting the small pouch tied within her waistband containing a portrait miniature of Dobie and two coins. The coins were not nearly enough to begin her new life in a new world. Now that there'd be no honest pay to collect from the *Maravilla*, how would she manage? How often did pirates collect their dues? More importantly, how would she earn her share? She didn't know the first thing about pillage and plunder. Nor would she ever rob or hurt innocent people.

"What about you, Elysen?"

Elyssa shook off her thoughts and shifted her gaze to Mac, a deckhand who'd become the closest thing to a friend on the merchant vessel. Namely because he wouldn't stop jabbering on to her about his sweetheart, Bridgette, and the puppy he'd given her. Mac called her by the only name he knew, the only name Dobie had given her.

"Why'd you choose a pirate's life?"

She couldn't tell him the truth. What if she put his life in danger, too?

"I figure I'm losing my wages staying with Captain Alonso. Why not take a chance?"

"Verily." Mac agreed, giving a good tug on the cap covering his bright red hair.

'Twasn't entirely a lie. But then she hadn't been given the choice to decide with which ship to cast her lot, either.

"Why'd you come, Mac? Joining a pirate crew, won't Bridgette find it dishonorable and dangerous?"

A dreamy smile spread across his freckled mug, reaching clear up to his sparkling green eyes. "I'd gladly hang for the chance to buy my bonny lass a gemstone necklace to lie across her bosom."

Talking about his girl always put Mac in good spirits, but it left Elyssa empty. What would it feel like to love someone that much? Would she ever know? Dobie didn't love her, not really. And try as she might, Elyssa couldn't foster anything more than tolerance, though she had hoped to love him some day. Just as her mother had her father.

She plucked the last piece of her supper into her mouth. The salted fish combined with the sticky air left her mouth as parched as a sun-baked plank of wood. A jack-tar broke open a cask of bumboo and she joined the others scrambling to dip their bowls and cups into the rum. The spicy-sweet drink, heavy on the nutmeg, quenched her thirst, but only after she double-dipped her bowl. 'Twas very good rum. Elyssa might dip her bowl thrice.

Lively music flowed from a fiddler and a few men burst into a sea shanty. Laughter, clapping, and the thumping of dancing boots added to the cheery noise. Indeed, these pirates knew how to have a merry time. Elyssa couldn't help but enjoy the revelry. Yet after the sixth, or was it the seventh, song, she moved to a quieter spot near the stern. To think.

Elyssa leaned on the railing. Wakes the boat left in the black water below whirred and frothed, reminding her how far she'd come from sitting in her father's drawing room with her needlework. Did she miss home? She wasn't sure. Yes, she missed Papa. Had made it a point to send him a letter at every port. But she didn't miss the pomp and circumstance expected from a young lady. Not now after masquerading as a boy. Not after witnessing firsthand the carousing of men after dark. So exciting, so exotic, these taverns they've visited in port. She longed to enjoy life without the constraints of social etiquette.

Men, they had freedoms. Women were expected to feast at the feet of their fathers and husbands, and be thankful. Subordinate, ornamental, quiet—that was not for Elyssa. Bless her father for she sorely tested his patience with her willful antics and talk of women in far off lands exercising their freedoms, establishing businesses and depending on no man. Her dream was to be one of them. Someday.

"Elysen, is it?"

She spun around and came face-to-face with her pirate *friend*. An ugly sneer crossed his even uglier mug.

"That yer real name, *boy*?"

Elyssa stiffened. He was definitely on to her. Careful not to show fear, she kept her voice low and steady. "'Tis the name I answer to."

"Iff'n ya want to keep it that way, lass, you'll answer to me, now." He stepped in close, pinning her between the rail and the wall of the poop deck. "Aye, I know yer secret. An' yer gonna do as I say lest I squeal. Ya know what they do to pullets on pirate ships?"

Shivers crawled over her spine at his nasty chuckle.

Her gaze shifted past him to the others singing, dancing, and drinking. How long before any of the men noticed the two of them shrouded in the shadows? And if she alerted the pirates, what beastly nightmare would await her? *What can I do?*

His smile slowly faded. "Hold still and don't make a peep." He grabbed the collar of her tunic and yanked her to him. His cracked lips smothered her mouth whilst his free hand groped at her backend. Elyssa gagged on his fetid tongue and struggled to be free of him. Grunting and grappling, she pushed and pounded against him to no avail. Her flesh smarted from his mauling hands, her neck cramped

from writhing. Unable and unwilling to breath, she slapped her palms against the wall again and again.
Dear Lord, help me!

CHAPTER 2

"By thunder, Kipp! What's that infernal noise?" Blackthorn slammed his fist upon the table serving as his desk. He'd been weighing options with his quartermaster and best mate. Though the *Maraville* provisions would get them by for another couple weeks or so, the supplies weren't enough. They had to decide whether to continue preying on the shipping lanes or chancing a friendly port to trade their newly acquired goods. But how could anyone make a decision with that consistent smacking against the outside wall?

"Sounds like the boys are scufflin' over another bad game of bones," Kipp said.

"We can't have these distractions." Blackthorn's mood soured. He hated distractions. "I want to make a decision tonight."

"Aye." Kipp finished off his cup of rum and stood. "We'll need to set a true course soon. I'll go break it up."

"Tell them they'll lose their passage if I'm disturbed again."

Kipp snorted. He knew Blackthorn would never carry out the threat and throw anyone overboard. At least not for such a minor infraction.

Blackthorn returned to adding the cargo items into his log book. The crates of fine fabrics from the merchant ship would fetch a hearty sum. Enough to stock up on provisions and let the lads drink until they saw a flock of moons. Assuming they risk dropping anchor. Even in friendly seaports there were those who would gladly collect the bounty on Blackthorn and his men. He chuckled to himself. And what a gracious bounty it was.

Blackthorn had no problem preying on unsuspecting vessels to keep his men and ship healthy. But he wasn't blind. Men like him were kings for only a short while. Eventually, he would meet his death for his crimes. Until then, he intended to uphold his oath of allegiance to the brotherhood.

His door slammed open. Kipp shoved Rathbone through the threshold, pulling along the young runt by his sleeve.

"What's this?" Blackthorn set down his quill and leaned back in his chair. This would be interesting. For Kipp to bring in these fellows whilst Blackthorn conducted his business, they'd had to have breached the articles they swore to.

"M' 'pologies, Capt'n," Rathbone said. He wisely kept his stare on the floor.

"Caught him takin' liberties on the lad," Kipp said.

Blackthorn crossed his arms over his chest. "Oh?"

Rathbone's head shot up. "No. He's mistaken." His mouth hardly moved as he spat out the words.

Kipp slowly shook his head. "No mistakin' where yer hands were, mate."

Rathbone began to speak, but Blackthorn held up a stern hand. He slid his gaze to the boy. The lad refused to make eye contact with anyone, but his eyes darted nervously about the room and his arms were wrapped soundly around his waist. Odd, the boy acted more like a scared…poppet.

Curse it! Could it be? A lass on board his ship. How did this happen?

"What's your name boy?" Blackthorn asked, trying to control the sudden anger threatening to explode.

"Elysen, sir."

Blackthorn had to strain to hear the girl. "Well then, Elysen, what do you have to say?"

"'Tis a misunderstanding, is all, sir."

"A misunderstanding. I see." No truths would be spoken in the present company. Just as well. 'Twas best to contain the situation.

Blast it! He flicked his quill on his desk, more than a little plagued by what this snake had done.

"Rathbone. You are aware you have violated Article Nine of the code, are you not?"

The wretch's jaw muscles worked feverishly. He'd been caught, and he knew what came next. He nodded once.

"Punishment for meddling with a boy," he paused to look at Rathbone's trifle, "or woman, is death."

Elysen let a tiny gasp slip.

Kipp gawked at the girl, realization had struck. "Shit." Blackthorn almost laughed at his friend. Almost. Everything had changed. The whole evening of planning had gone down the pissdale. They now had a very real problem.

"Now tell me again, your name, lass."

"El—Elyssa. Elyssa Calhoun Montgomery."

The lass watched as Blackthorn rose from his seat, but when her eyes collided with his, she quickly looked away. He moved in front of her, and he could swear she would melt from fear.

"You've got much to explain, lass." The poor thing trembled.

"Kipp," Blackthorn said. "Shackle Rathbone below."

"But, Capt'n."

"Not now, Rathbone. You can explain yourself to the men tomorrow."

"Come on, ya bastard." Rathbone struggled against Kipp's grip on his arm, growling until Kipp poked a pistol into his side.

Blackthorn swiped the small cap off the lass and pulled away the scarf wrapped around her head, throwing them both to his desk. The short braid of hair fell into a long auburn plait down her back.

"What the devil were you thinking, boarding my ship as a lad? Do you have any idea what will become of you now? Do you know what harm awaits you? What terrible torture... Look at me when I address you."

Eyes of brown, as rich in color as his finest rum, finally met his. Now that she gave him the full effect of her fair face, he found her a fetching little pigeon. Tears spilled down her bronzed cheeks. Aye, and she knew well enough her predicament.

"'Twasn't my wish, sir." Her bottom lip quivered. "I'd have stayed on the *Maravilla* had your man Rathbone not threatened to give me away."

"Did he?" That rotten bugger. 'Twas certain he had nasty plans for the lass. Probably aimed to toss her to the sea before anyone became wise to the girl. Blackthorn never did care for the bastard. Not since that incident involving a tavern wench back in Port Royal. He knew deep in his gut Rathbone had something to do with her death. Rathbone would get his due. Blackthorn would see to it.

"How is it you are disguised as a boy on a merchant vessel?"

"I had no choice. I couldn't let Papa down." Her voice hitched up, frantic as if she didn't want to disappoint her father even now out in the middle of the Caribbean Sea. "Papa needed my help. I would be a good daughter. I didn't want him to worry. He was always worrying."

"You're father made you do this?" He waved his hand over her attire.

"No."

"Speak up, child."

She rubbed her arm, hesitant to speak further. When she would say no more, he raised his brow for encouragement. "No. Dobie did. My husband."

"Husband?" *Intriguing.*

"I'd do anything for Papa." The words began to pour out of her, as if she were confessing her sins instead of explaining herself. "Even marrying a banker's wayward son to satisfy his debts. The merger allowed Papa to keep his shipping business. He won't have to wonder any longer whether he can feed my younger sisters. Lord Montgomery was ever so generous."

The name suddenly became familiar. "Lord Samuel Montgomery?"

She nodded

"*The* Lord Samuel Montgomery?"

She nodded once more.

Daughter-in-law to the very wealthy Lord Samuel Montgomery? Here on his ship? Sounds of gold coins clamored in his ears. What price would she fetch for her safe return? This certainly made his evening more complicated. Blackthorn's temples throbbed from the makings of a royal headache. And still the lass had yet to tell him everything. "This doesn't explain why you are masking as a boy."

She wrung her hands, in and over, over and in, shifting her weight from foot to foot, unable to stand still. Fidgety little chit.

"Dobie wanted to open his own exchange in the West Indies. But Lord Montgomery wouldn't finance his trip, not one penny. He insisted Dobie was too irresponsible and careless." Blackthorn would agree, careless with his woman. What kind of fool dresses up his wife and drags her along across an ocean, putting her virtue and life in danger?

"'Twas one reason he thought I'd be a good match for his son as a sensible wife. Angry, Dobie decided he didn't need his father's help. He'd make his own way, and once in

San Juan, he'd get by on his name. I begged him to take me with him. I couldn't let Lord Montgomery renege on his settlement with Papa. I just couldn't."

"And your husband agreed?"

"Well, no. I promised to find work in bookkeeping, or as a serving girl in a tavern, anything. I'd give him anything to help build his wealth. I'd do whatever it took, just so he'd bring me."

Blackthorn admired the love and loyalty she had for her family, risking her life for those closest to her. Not unlike that of the brethren. Yet, he didn't feel her husband had her best interest in mind, only his.

"And so he signed you up as a seaman on a Spanish bucket." He couldn't hide his disgust if he wanted to. "How did you keep your secret? Surely you've had your monthly courses?" Perhaps he should have been more delicate in asking such a personal question. But he never was much for dancing around proper etiquette when he wanted answers. Besides, he found the reddening in her cheeks curiously alluring.

"I, um, I haven't had my, um, courses. Dobie thought if I worked as hard as a man, drank as hard as a man, and want to really be a man, my body would follow suit."

'Twas more likely because she was half starved. What a skinny thing. A woman should have more meat on those curves. That's the way Blackthorn liked them. Maybe he should have Hobbs whip her up some lobscouse.

"Dobie said I'd need to pretend to fall ill should, um, it happen."

Dobie. Dobie. Ugh, Blackthorn didn't much care for this lackey. Immature, selfish, neglectful, swab. "Where is Dobie now?" Because Blackthorn would like to have a word with this lout.

She averted her gaze to the farthest corner of his cabin. "He's dead. Fell from the yardarm, broke his neck."

Blackthorn drew a long breath. "I see."

He had enough problems. Now he had a potentially profitable widow on board. What was he going to do with her? Where would he keep her? 'Twas bad luck to have a woman aboard a ship, or so the tales go. Despite the claims otherwise, most of the *Sanctum* men would never hurt a woman. Still, they were a superstitious lot and he couldn't let her loose on his ship and risk something happening to her. Especially once the men passed their judgment on Rathbone. Nay, this did not bode well for Blackthorn. He had little choices, and Blackthorn hated that.

"Are you going to kill me?"

Blackthorn tried not to smirk, but he did anyhow. The reputation of a pirate afforded him many advantages. He'd be telling false truths if he said he didn't enjoy seeing her squirm. He circled around her, only a hair's breadth from touching her.

"Nay, lass. I'm not going to kill you. But I haven't decided what I shall do with you, either." He bent to whisper in her ear. "Though a few savory ideas come to mind."

He rounded back in front of her and peered down. Her tunic hung close to her body. The urge to see if she wore bindings to help her look more like a boy was too strong. He hooked a finger into the collar. She squeezed her eyes shut. The poor lass. He shouldn't toy with her so. She trembled something awful. Never mind that. The cur that he was, he wanted to see what wares she hid. And he wasn't disappointed. Even with the binds tight, her breasts brimmed over the top. How uncomfortable she must be. The rapid rise and fall of her chest reminded him of a petrified rabbit trying desperately not to be seen by a passing fox. Oh, but this fox saw her. And he was beginning to think she might be a tasty morsel.

"Please, Captain Blackthorn." The lass opened her eyes. "Please, have mercy. I'd rather you just kill me than lay a hand on me."

"Dear, Elyssa. You flatter yourself. I said nothing about taking you." Though he was well into imagining so. What pleasure would a lass bring who dares to willingly cast herself among pirates? He would be most interested to find out. If he were a lesser man, he'd already have her stripped of her clothes. Damned moral restraints. Sometimes, just sometimes, he'd wished he could live up to the lecherous reputation and false tales bestowed upon him by the fearful. He wouldn't of course. Never would he take from a woman's virtue what she wouldn't freely give. But her jewels and coin, well now, that's another matter.

"Besides, I'm not the merciful type." His statement didn't bring ease to her stiff posture. Wisely so. She was still prey.

"What would you have me do, then? Can I prove to you my keep?" She realized all too late the implications of her suggestion.

"Tantalizing offer." He finally moved away, giving her breathing room before she fainted from lack of air.

Quickly, she amended. "I can mend ropes and sails."

"Mending ropes and sail will not be nearly enough to remedy the serious position you have put me in, lass. No doubt the entire ship knows about you by now. Understand, I can't let you leave this room. This is inconvenient, you see, because this cabin is also where I take my solitude...and sleep. So, dear girl, you have imposed upon me greatly."

Worry knitted her brow and she gnawed on her plump bottom lip. Ripe lips. Lips that beckoned to be kissed. Blazes! *Back on task, man. You've more important matters to chaw over than her mouth.*

"I understand," she said.

"Nay, I don't think you do." He perched upon the edge of his table. "The moment you stepped into my quarters, you lost your freedom." The more he thought about it, the more annoyed he became, sharing his cabin with a woman. One he wasn't even bedding. Bah! And how the hell was he supposed to conduct business with her there? Ah yes, he was growing ever more agitated. "Consider yourself my prisoner."

"P-prisoner?"

White teeth chewed upon her lip again. *Look away.* He didn't, of course, and that rankled him further. "Aye, and as such, you will indulge to my whims. A fair trade for what would await you outside that door." Nothing wrong with putting more fear into the lass lest she decide to do something rash.

"But—"

"Tut!" He walked around his desk and sat. Dipping his quill in the inkwell, he went back to cataloguing cargo in his log book. Without looking up, he gave his first instruction. "You may remove your binds now."

"Beg your pardon?"

He pointed with his quill. "You're bindings, remove them. You've no need for them any longer." He went back to jotting on the paper. "I won't have you pretending to be someone you're not in my presence. You should be relieved."

Relieved? Elyssa was anything but relieved. She was trapped in this cabin with a pirate captain, one who wanted her to disrobe. He said he wouldn't kill or rape her and, strangely, she believed him. Why, she did not know. Perhaps it was because he could've already done so. She'd heard tales of pirates keeping female prisoners for their enjoyment. Most of those stories ended with *and she was never heard from again*. Elyssa might find out firsthand if there was any truth to the stories.

Captain Blackthorn looked up from his book and scowled. "That wasn't a suggestion, lass. Remove your bindings."

"I can't."

"Oh? Why is that?"

"The knots are in the back." Elyssa hated to say it. What a terrible mess this would lead to.

The corner of his mouth twitched. "Remove your tunic," he said, putting down his quill and rising.

"Must I?"

"Do you want to risk my good nature with fruitless questions? No? Remove the tunic or I shall do it for you."

In the last several months, Elyssa had faced monumental decisions. Though the choices were hers, they weren't really choices at all. They had always been made for the good of another. So it seemed that way even now. She crossed her arms down, grabbed the hem of her shirt, and tugged the fabric up and over. The cool air landed upon her bare shoulders. Goose skin puckered across her flesh. Was it because of the draft landing upon her naked skin, or the heated expression passing over the captain's amused face?

"Turn around," he said, taking her tunic and tossing it to the table.

She did as he bade and faced the door. His salty scent filled her nose as he neared from behind, reminding her of the gentle rains she so loved rolling in from the sea. Elyssa suspected he was no gentle rain, but rather a boisterous storm. And yet, she breathed him in deep.

"Christ. Who made these knots? They're dreadful."

"Dob—"

"The lubber knew nothing about knots."

The captain worked and tugged on the bonds. 'Twas such an intimate act. Undressing should be done in the company of a husband, not a stranger. Still, with the pressure of his fingers working on the cloth at her back, her heart picked up pace.

"By gads, these will never come loose. Shit. Hold still."

The moment the blade touched her skin she froze.

"Be very still, do you understand?"

She nodded.

He worked the knife slowly up her spine, slicing through the fabric nearly to the top. She exhaled when he removed the dagger. And with a final tug, he ripped the bindings away, exposing her fully.

Her breasts fell free and her clammy skin chilled in the brisk relief. She could finally take a full breath. And would have done so had the door not flung open.

Elyssa shrieked. For a full moment, Mister Kipp, wide-eyed and shaken by her scream, stared, his mouth hanging agape. She flung her arms over her bosom and spun around smacking into the captain's hard chest.

His throaty chuckle rumbled in her ear. How dare he laugh. Mister Kipp got quite an eyeful. She was mortified with embarrassment and Captain Blackthorn found it all entertaining. She should be teeming with resentment. 'Twas his doing, making her disrobe. But the moment he wrapped his arm around her shoulder, pulling her close, well, her mind muddled. His hold, the warmth seeping in from his arm, the gentle squeeze, confused her. Heat from his calloused hand burned upon her flesh. And she liked it. Such foolhardy thoughts. He was a dangerous man, and she his prisoner. She shouldn't lose sight of that.

"I think it wise to knock, eh, Mister Kipp?"

"So it seems, Capt'n. My deepest apologies to ya, and to ye, miss."

Elyssa could only nod, not wanting to look Mister Kipp in the face, as much for not wanting to move from the captain's embrace as for humiliation.

"Remember that French bucket we claimed last month?" Captain Blackthorn said. "If I recall, we acquired one pompous traveler's chest of fine dresses and under things, no?"

"Ah, yes. I'll never forget that cat-claw. Couldn't stuff a gag in her vicious yap fast enough." Mister Kipp chuckled. "Ya be wantin' me to bring it up?"

"Aye. Mrs. Montgomery will be staying in my cabin for the rest of the voyage."

"I reckon that'll be a bid for trouble, mate."

"So was that cat-claw, yet you still managed a dalliance with her."

"Aye, that I did." A crooked smile hitched up Mister Kipp's cheek. "Then I couldn't get rid of the fair piece. Trouble, I say."

"Verily. No more trouble than I can handle."

Bedad. She was practically stark naked and these two were reminiscing. Elyssa cleared her throat.

The captain smiled down to her, his eyes migrating to her breasts she squished to hide. Though she didn't hear Mister Kipp's response, she did hear the latch of the hatch door closing over her pounding heartbeat.

"The quartermaster is usually the first to handle the spoils of quarry. 'Tis fitting, I suppose, that Mister Kipp witnessed your prizes before his captain."

She gulped down the chirrup caught in her throat.

"Do not fret, lass, I'll be a gentleman...for the time being."

His arm dropped away and she suddenly felt the vulnerability she should have had all along.

Captain Blackthorn handed back her shirt. "I'll return straightaway." Without another word, he left.

He'd been gone long enough for her to begin to understand her dire circumstance, but not so long to know how to handle it. Those crazy feelings of attraction, they appeared from nowhere, throwing her common sense to the wind. She was no driveling goosecap. She was a man, er, woman. She would make her way out of this mess. She *would* make it to San Juan, she *would* use her newly acquired Montgomery name, and she *would* be all right. But for now she had to take it breath by breath. And curb her attraction for Captain Blackthorn.

Upon his return, he set a bucket of rainwater on the floor. Mister Kipp followed with a large trunk. The quartermaster added it to other trunks set against the shelves securing the captain's books, navigational instruments, and drinking cups.

"The lads are stirred up," Mister Kipp said.

"Imagine they are," the captain said. "I'll be out momentarily to address them."

Mister Kipp bowed his head to Elyssa and winked before leaving once again. She'd never be able to look at the man again without heat flushing her cheeks.

"'Tis late," the captain said. "Bathe and take your rest." He handed her a rag. "You may sleep in my bunk."

Sleeping in a pirate's bed? Elyssa glanced at the thin pallet against the wall. Scandalous. There was no other word for her situation. Her troubles burrowed deeper and deeper. *Come now, Elyssa. For months you've been sleeping in close quarters with dozens of strange men.* Ah, but *as* a man. There was a distinct difference. She should be pleased to lie on a mattress again, meager as it was. But would she lie alone? Or would Captain Blackthorn have immoral intentions in mind?

She looked back to the man who would keep her and was startled to find him staring. No, not staring, gazing. Damn, what was it about his eyes that had her drawn to him? She couldn't break away from their hold, nor did she want to.

The faintest of smiles flitted across the captain's lips. "On the morrow, you may pick out a dress from the chest." He rolled up a map and packed up his journal. "And do wash that dreadful hair of yours."

Instinctively, her hand flew to her head. Her plaited hair crinkled to the touch.

"If I'm to accommodate you by keeping you safe in my quarters, you will accommodate me by making yourself presentable." He scooped up his rum bottle and turned to leave.

"Captain Blackthorn," she called.

He paused at the door without looking back.

"Thank you."

"Don't thank me yet, Mrs. Montgomery. I've yet to determine what I shall do with you."

CHAPTER 3

Blackthorn had hardly stepped out of his cabin before the men crowded in. They peppered him with questions. Angry voices carried on about the trickery of a woman sneaking on board the *Sanctum*. Others were curious about who the lass was. Most were anxious to pass judgment on Rathbone. A handful called for justice. Justice for who was debatable and so Blackthorn left the men with one clear order. No harm was to come to the woman lest the wretch meet with a bullet between the eyes. He didn't feel the threat was necessary except for the few that might be sympathetic to Rathbone's plight.

The men parted and Blackthorn made his way below to the galley. He needed a quiet place to finish off his rum and think about his predicament. He should be deciding on a course, making a firm decision on a port or to continue pirating. Instead, his mind wandered to the delight in his cabin. By God, what he wouldn't give to watch her rub that rag across her wet, naked skin.

He smiled. He'd have to thank Kipp for barging into his quarters. Blackthorn had nearly come undone when the lass spun into him. How soft and warm her flesh. Her breasts rounding over her arm in an attempt to hide them made his mouth water. 'Twas a terrible shame to have a naked woman in his cabin and not be able to enjoy her.

"Yer one lucky bastard." Kipp ducked into the galley and took a seat across from him at the table.

"How so?"

"A woman, alone in yer quarters, in the middle of the Caribbean." He sat down two cups and a fresh flagon of spirit. "Blimey. A man couldn't ask for a better blessing. And might I add she has blessings of her own." Kipp whistled.

"Aha, who's the lucky one, my friend?"

They shared a laugh, but harsh reality kept Blackthorn from enjoying their raillery.

"She's a blessing, all right, or a curse. That pretty pullet happens to be Lord Samuel Montgomery's daughter-in-law."

"*The* Lord Samuel Montgomery? Ya don't say." Kipp poured them each a drink. Midway through pouring his cup, Blackthorn's meaning dawned upon him. "Oh." Kipp smirked. "Now I get ya. Don't want to spoil the goods, eh?"

"That's right, mate. Montgomery might pay a king's ransom for her safe return. Wouldn't want to taint the leverage."

"Puts us in a bit of a dilemma, don't it?"

"Aye." More so than Kipp might realize. Years ago, before Edward Flynn wiled his way into a commission in the governor's palace on New Providence, Flynn trolled the same waters as Blackthorn. And when the *Sanctum* poached the mighty fine Spanish galleon busting with gold Flynn had been chasing, well, Flynn swore revenge.

"Flynn finds out we have the lass, we may never get that King's Pardon."

"He'll look for any reason to deny me, that you can be sure. Flynn will, without fail, charge us with kidnapping."

"The bastard will put into the hands of every pardoned pirate a letter of marque to kill us." Kipp took a healthy gulp from his cup and swiped the dribble from his mouth with his shirtsleeve.

"Nay, he'd rather we be taken alive so he can hang me himself."

"Ya'd think being blood kin would have bearing."

Blackthorn snorted. "My being the bastard son of a Rear Admiral does not bind us by blood, Kipp. 'Tis just another reason my brother would gladly see to my death. Never mind. Flynn knows I'll stick to my word. I'll leave his waters and trade commerce alone. Should he grant the *Sanctum* clemency, of course."

"And if yer man Christensen fails to secure the pardon?"

"I'll declare war with Flynn."

Kipp raised his cup in a toast. "Damn the Governor. May the devil place a plague on his scurvy head."

Blackthorn smiled and raised his cup in turn.

"Ya trust this Christensen?" Kipp asked.

He scratched at the stubble on his chin. Robert Christensen was like a brother to him. As young lads, they trained and fought as naval infantry during the War of Spanish Succession. Comrades had claimed the two were formidable, striking down enemies on the battlefield in synchronized precision, and always watching one another's back. 'Twasn't enough for Christensen or for himself. Neither wanted to sail around the West Indies waiting for the next land battle. With a little friendly competition, they vowed to become skilled as master seamen, as well. It was said they would both rise to the top ranks. That was before an unfortunate accident stripped Blackthorn of all he'd worked hard for and removed him from the Royal Navy permanently.

"Commodore Christensen will do what he can, but his loyalty lies with the crown."

"A fool's errand, I say."

Blackthorn agreed. Either way, reprieve or no reprieve. Only the decision mattered. He'd long since grown weary of the cruising trade. If he couldn't reap the rewards of his roving commission, then he'd go out a pirate's legend. And he'd take Flynn with him.

"What course do we take, Capt'n?"

"Set a heading for New Providence and pray we don't run into too much trouble in port. Samuel Montgomery is a Lord Proprietor, owning much of the island. He has an office in Nassau. We send Montgomery's officer our terms and his daughter-in-law's condition—nothing more."

"Bold. Crafty. Just like ya, Bran."

"A man's got to make his way with what he's been given, mate. And God, or the Devil, has given me a fetching nymph to line my coffers."

The middle watch bell cleaved through the silence and caught on the midnight breeze. Black water below rolled and stirred from the *Sanctum's* hull. The moonless night cloaked Blackthorn's ship making for an odd sense of suspension somewhere between time and the sea.

Across the chasm there was no distinction between the water and sky. He sighed, comforted by the lonely and dark void. That empty place, meant for him, understood him.

Exhaustion tugged upon his limbs and his back ached. He was getting too old for this shit. 'Twas time to retire.

Ah, but the lass, Elyssa, was in his cabin. He'd left her hours ago, gave her the privacy required to bathe—as a gentleman should. Though he was far from a gentleman these days, he was no boorish cad either. No reason he couldn't give the lady the decency a woman deserved. Thoughts of her wet, bare skin danced through his mind once more. He suspected she'd clean up nicely. Anticipation of seeing her chased his exhaustion away. What treat awaited him in his quarters—his *private* quarters. His cabin had been invaded by a wayward chit on a fanciful adventure. He growled. Perhaps he should sleep on the deck tonight. Piss on that. No woman was going to run him out of his only place of exile on the sloop.

He took a final pull from the flagon of rum, his third this night, and pushed off the rail.

Blackthorn entered his cabin in a wash of light. Every blasted lantern had been lit, their flames turned up high. Didn't the lass know safety could not always be found in the light? Her seaman clothes, scrubbed clean of shipboard grime, lay draped over the chests to dry. Was that rose petals he smelled? Yes, he definitely smelled roses. She must have found perfume in the Frenchwoman's trunk. He fancied the floral fragrance. Reminded him of the glittery parties filled with festive music, courtly dancing, and coy smiles. Every young soldier such as himself had been hopeful to steal a chaste kiss from a sweet young lady. The floral scent harkened memories of his youthful luck in wooing a lass or two.

He let his eyes wander to Elyssa curled in his bed. The sheet tucked clear up to her chin. Heigho, the thin cloth did nothing to hide the dips and swells of her body underneath. Wisps of tawny locks swept around her peaceful face and fanned out on his pillow. Blazes. Seeing her there, so vulnerable, so intimate, caused a stir in a lamentably underused spot in his trousers. Sweet and tempting. He realized he hadn't moved away from the door. Damn! 'Twould be a long night if he kept staring.

Blackthorn took a seat and propped his feet on his desk, careful not to make too much noise. Not that he feared disturbing her sleep. Nay, he knew well enough Elyssa Calhoun Montgomery was wide awake.

Elyssa awoke to an empty cabin, to which she sent up a relieved prayer of thanks. She sat up, stretched her arms upward easing her tight muscles, and yawned. The last couple of hours had been the best sleep she'd had since becoming a man. But it hadn't come quickly. Pretending to be sleeping when Captain Blackthorn returned in the middle of the night had proved difficult. She had stolen glances of the pirate through her eyelashes. Not too many as he, too, watched her. She refused to sleep not knowing the man's intentions. If he attacked her, she'd go down fighting. The small dagger she had found hidden in one of the Frenchwoman's boots allayed some threads of vulnerability. But the handle dug into her side causing her a fit of discomfort. Such as it was, he just sat in his chair. At times, she couldn't be sure, but he seemed to drift away in thought, contemplating, a little sad, perhaps. Criminy, she thought the man would never fall asleep. Eventually he did. The moment his chin dipped forward she knew he had slipped into slumber.

She had studied him without reservation. His arms crossed over an expansive chest. Long lean legs strained against his trousers. His thick hair bereft of a bind rested just below his shoulders. No visible mars or oddities to his face. So unlike Dobie with his aquiline nose and pocked cheeks. The captain was handsome indeed. *Remember your place, silly girl. A pirate's prisoner.*

The floorboard cooled her bare feet as Elyssa stood. She tucked the knife under the mattress and padded to the trunks. The Frenchwoman had quite a selection of luxurious gowns and shoes that surely cost a small fortune. 'Twas no doubt the reason Captain Blackthorn kept the chest. She picked out a delightful blue damask *contouche* with silk ribbons. 'Twas the simplest gown she could find.

A bath, privacy, a bed, and now a fine dress. One thing for certain, the captain showed her a batch of kindness. Would telling him how grateful she was extend his good nature towards her? She hoped so.

Dressing took quite a bit of time without aid. Nevertheless, even after pulling the front laces of the French corset tight, she could breathe much easier in the fitted gown than the torturous binds she wore as a lad. After fiddling with her hair and tying it with a ribbon, there was nothing left to do but wait for Captain Blackthorn. She nearly gnawed her fingernails down to nubs when he finally returned.

His brow hitched up, accompanied by an appreciative smile. "Mrs. Montgomery, permit me to say you look much better as a woman than a mangy boy. A real feast upon the eyes."

Elyssa's cheeks warmed. Seems she was always in a state of blushing. She bowed her head. "Thank you, Captain Blackthorn."

Gruff shouting carried in from outside. The captain tilted his head to give a listen.

"Yes, well, perhaps too womanly. I may have made an error in insisting you clothe this way, but there's no time for you to change now."

Quite suddenly, Elyssa felt like a dressed dish to be served up to a horde of half-starved warriors.

A knock was followed by Mister Kipp's announcement.

"Enter," Captain Blackthorn said.

"Capt'n, the men are restless and Rathbone is…" Mister Kipp's gaze landed upon her. A silly grin reached his eyes. "Blister me. May my deadlights go blind now that they've seen something as lovely as ye, my lady."

She was fairly certain that was a compliment meant with the highest esteem. Her embarrassment in Mister Kipp's presence abated, but only somewhat.

"Just as ravishing clothed as—"

"Kipp." Blackthorn cleared his throat. "You were saying?"

Elyssa's cheeks surely would burst into flames. Lord, she must get over this mortification before she burned to a cinder. He meant no harm by his flattery. 'Twasn't as if she were a coddled damsel. Far worse vulgar conversations were rampant among her fellow seamen on the *Maraville*.

"Oh, yes, my apologies. Rathbone is topside."

"Good. Give us a moment."

Mister Kipp nodded and stepped back into the din of fitful men.

"Be forewarned, lass." Blackthorn walked over to a trunk. He fished a key from his pocket and unlocked the metal padlock sealing the chest. "It will become volatile out there. Our articles are strictly followed, and as you know, Rathbone faces death for his poor judgment. The only reason the men are to decide punishment is due to your deceit." Dropping the key back into his pocket, he then retrieved a flintlock from the arsenal inside and shoved it into his belt. The gun wasn't a good sign. He expected trouble. "You shall stay by my side while the proceedings take place. Are we clear?"

"Yes, Captain Blackthorn. Quite clear." He may have to pry her off his side with an iron crow.

"Very well. Let us go. And try not to look so attractive."

She didn't believe acting invisible as she did on the merchant ship would work now. "How am I supposed to do that? Hack and spit and grab my tallywags?" *Attractive? He finds me attractive?*

The captain chuckled at her boorish talk and opened the door. A breath of sun-baked air rushed in around him, bussing her face and lifting the ribbons of her gown. He stepped out, but before she could follow, he surprised her with an extended hand. She hesitated, staring at the calloused pads of his fingers. Another simple but courteous act. She was beginning to think Captain Blackthorn was a gentleman.

He led her over the threshold and instantly the angry shouts and accusations died away. The captain pressed close behind her as they climbed the ladder to the poop deck. His proximity felt a bit improper, if not possessive, and she admitted she rather liked it. Given her circumstance, of course.

Elyssa took her place between the captain and Mister Kipp.

Waves of mixed reactions from the crew smashed into her. She squirmed under snarls and smiles alike, both sets looked ready to eat her alive. Across the crowd of dirty faces, she picked out Mac. She saw the hurt of betrayal in his eyes, etched into his frown. His disappointment impaled her. She valued his friendship more than she realized. Regret was terrible to swallow. She mouthed *I'm sorry*, but he shook his head and looked away.

Whispers turned into jeers and trifling suggestions.

"Ain't she a pretty dainty bit."

"Aye, a real beauty, I'd say."

"I'd give my fightin' arm for a romp with this one, I would."

Criminy, she failed quite miserably at looking unattractive. Elyssa hacked, coughed, hacked again, and spat to the floor. She swore she heard the captain chuckle. He didn't hold back his grin, either. The rest of the crew looked at her curiously, but only for a moment and quickly returned to heckling.

"Mind your manners, men," Captain Blackthorn said. "Now that you've *met* Mrs. Montgomery, we need to get to the matter at hand. I trust you understand Rathbone had been caught assaulting the lady."

Rathbone sent her icy stabs of hate and she had a good mind to switch places with Captain Blackthorn.

"Cast yer eyes," Rathbone hollered. "This bunter been livin' among tarry-breeks, foolin' the lot of 'em." He pointed to the recent *Maraville* crewmen. "You and you and you. She been lyin' to ya."

"Shut yer trap," Mister Kipp said.

"Now she's tricked the rest of ya. Made ya all fools. A woman! Don't that make ya madder than 'ellfire?"

"Rathbone."

There was no mistaking Captain Blackthorn's tone. There'd be hell to pay if the man did not quiet down. Elyssa wished he'd heed the warning. But Rathbone hardly acknowledged his captain had spoken.

"She should be the one tried, the bitch. Why is *she* 'ere?"

Crewman bobbed their heads, wanting answers. Hollers for her head, for the injustice she had caused, grew louder. Elyssa rubbed her neck. She did not want to know how a hempen rope would feel against her throat. One man argued the bad luck they'd surely suffer having a woman on board. They would need to make reparations to the sea and reverse any ill fate.

Suggestions of what to do with her sent a surge of panic through her veins. She gauged the distance to the ship's railing. Would she make it, throwing herself overboard before any of the pirate crew caught her? Not likely.

"Quiet, Rathbone," Captain Blackthorn warned again.

"The devil woman tempted me."

"What? No!" Elyssa couldn't believe what she was hearing. Rathbone was out of his mind. "I did no such thing." Elyssa stepped to the rail, pleading to the men below. "He's lying." She turned to Mister Kipp. "You saw what happened. Tell them he's lying."

"I ain't lyin'," Rathbone spat.

"Quiet, I said!" Captain Blackthorn's jaw locked tight.

"Devil woman!"

Captain Blackthorn drew his pistol, aiming it squarely between Rathbone's eyes.

Dear lord! Terror balled in Elyssa's chest.

Mister Kipp elbowed Rathbone in his mug. Blood trickled from his nose. "Respect yer capt'n, maggot."

Rathbone's shackled hands flew to his snout. His fiery gaze snapped up from the blood staining his fingers to his superiors, but he saved an especially hideous glare for Elyssa.

Captain Blackthorn slowly lowered his flintlock. Still facing Rathbone, he addressed his crew. "Mrs. Montgomery's reasons for being here are her own." He turned to his men. "She is under no fault that I am not directly handling." He wrapped his hand around her arm, his fingers digging uncomfortably into her flesh, and pulled her to stand just behind him. "She will be punished accordingly."

Captain Blackthorn was right. The shipboard trial had become volatile. Why didn't it occur to her that she, too, would face penalty from the crew? What did the captain have planned for her now? Whatever it was, she decided she'd fare better with him than be at the mercy of a handful of superstitious pirates.

"What say you regarding Rathbone?"

The pirates looked among themselves waiting for one of their own to speak. One by one, they deliberated.

"Don't seem right to kill 'im."

"Aye. The lass shouldn't a put herself here."

"But he shouldn't a placed a hand on her, no how."

"I say strap 'im to the guns and cut 'im loose next chance we get."

Many agreed with the last statement, satisfied with the idea.

"Right then," Captain Blackthorn said. "If no one disagrees...Rathbone, the *Sanctum* has spoken. You shall be rove to a gun and flayed with twenty-five lashes, then chained in the bilge." He leaned in close to the wretch. "Best be glad the boys spared you. I might not have been so forgiving."

"Nor would I, ya worthless louse," Mister Kipp added. "But don't ya fret. I got a cane made just for a good drubbin'. Make ya cry like a wee babe."

Captain Blackthorn smiled and winked before stepping back.

Mister Kipp prodded the condemned man forward. Despite the gun poking him in his ribs, Rathbone paused in front of Elyssa. A guttural growl rumbled from his snarled mouth. "You'll pay for this, bitch."

A shiver skittered up her spine. Lord, help her should she ever be caught alone with him again. He would kill her, of that she believed.

Captain Blackthorn stepped between them. "I doubt that, mate. Careful you don't threaten Mrs. Montgomery again lest I pass my own judgment upon you. Understand?"

Captain Blackthorn would do that for her? Protect her? *Isn't that what he's been doing?* The implication of his actions suddenly became clear.

Rathbone's narrowed scowl shifted from the captain to Elyssa and back again to the captain, but he said nothing.

"Move ahead." Mister Kipp grabbed Rathbone by the shoulder and shoved him forward.

"Come Mrs. Montgomery. A flogging is no place for a woman."

CHAPTER 4

Upon returning to the relative safety of his cabin, Elyssa gathered her courage. The door latch clicked and she whirled around to confront the captain. "You are a man of decency, Captain Blackthorn, not a loathsome rogue."

"Oh?"

"Yes. You've shown me undeserving kindness that most would not. Dare I say you are a gentleman."

"My mercy is fleeting."

"So it seems. You are unscrupulous leaving me to wonder what you will do with me."

"I've been accused of worse, little one. And not without truth to support the claims."

"Do you want to know what I think?" She cocked an eyebrow, testing him. "I think you have no intention of punishing me. I think you haven't any idea what to do with me."

"Dear lady. That is where you are wrong. I *have* decided what I will do with you and I am anxious to administer my decision."

By the look of his curling smile, Elyssa was in for some bedevilment.

"If I am to give up my privacy to you for the coming weeks, you will be my personal valet."

"A manservant?"

"Appropriate, wouldn't you agree? You've been parading around as a lad, you should have no trouble with seeing to my needs. Should I need a shave, you will shave me. Should my cup be empty, you will fill it. Should my tunic get a tear, you will mend it."

These demands, 'twas nothing she hadn't done for her father. She was making off like a thief.

His eyes darkened as they pierced clean through her. "Should I need to bathe…"

"To…bathe?" Did that squeak come from her or did the captain have a mouse in his cabin?

He chuckled, but his stare did not lighten with his mirth. "Aye. And I'm long past due for a good scrubbing." He plucked his shirt out and gave himself a sniff. "When was the last time I bathed?" Looking to the ceiling and scratching his chin, he pretended to be thinking the matter over, making a mockery of the whole idea.

"Oh no, Captain Blackthorn. You seem very clean."

"I should call for a tub to be prepared now." He pulled his tunic off.

Holy Mother of…

The balmy temperature in the room heated up and Elyssa had the sudden urge to fan herself. Never in her life had she seen such smooth, taut flesh. She didn't know what perfection looked like, but this had to be close. Dobie's torso, though not terribly flabby, had been less defined. He hardly ever held her, yet when he did she didn't quite fit in his embrace. She was left cold, not warm the way she thought a husband's embrace should be.

She wanted to touch Captain Blackthorn, feel his sun-bronzed chest under her fingertips. Drag them down over the ridges of his abdomen.

Elyssa! What has gotten into you? Why did she keep having these wanton thoughts? *Control yourself. You mustn't play with fire.*

"Sir. I really don't think you need—" She flinched as a strident scream broke beyond the cabin door. Another such cry quickly followed.

Captain Blackthorn sighed. "I'm afraid the luxury of a bath will have to wait. I must oversee Rathbone's flogging. A captain's duty, as it were."

She sighed a breath of relief at her luck. 'Twould be compromising at best to bathe a stranger. Surely with a pirate, trouble came tenfold.

He slipped back into his tunic. She swallowed a disappointed whimper. This must be what it felt like for a child eyeing a honey cake in the baker's window. She could ogle the morsel, but she would not get to sample the confection. *Ah, well. 'Tis for the best.*

"But never you mind, Mrs. Montgomery." He adjusted his sash holding his pistol at his waist, making sure the gun was secure. "You've not earned a reprieve. I will get that bath."

Damn the luck.

He paused at the door. "We'll dine first. Aye. It will be a splendid evening."

Blackthorn shouldn't have toyed with the lass. 'Twas an obnoxious thing to suggest she bathe him. Terrible and tantalizing. He hadn't meant it. Not really. But when he removed his shirt, he saw a spark of desire light in her eyes and he couldn't control himself. For a moment, just a moment, he thought to undress further. He delighted in watching her squirm.

Delighted even now as she *still* squirmed, fidgeting in her seat across the table from him.

Hobbs, the ship's cook, sat down a tray of pork and cabbage. He forked a piece of the meat to serve.

Blackthorn raised his hand to stop the cook. "The lady will be serving me tonight."

Hobbs snickered. "Earnin' her keep, eh? Gotta a turtle in the galley be needin' butcherin' if ya be wantin' to give 'er somethin' to do, Capt'n."

"'Fraid not, Hobbs. She'll be busy attending to me."

"Ah." He gave Blackthorn a wink. "Tough bein' Capt'n, eh?"

Blackthorn would gladly trade places with Hobbs. The burden of handling the lives of his entire crew, whether they'd find freedom or death, made him weary. Each man's fate was his responsibility and the weight he carried grew heavier with every passing day. And now this woman...

"Take your leave, Hobbs."

The moment the door closed, the lass rose and served up a heaping plate of food, leaving little on the tray.

"This food is meant to be shared, Mrs. Montgomery."

"I'm not terribly hungry." She topped off his cup and returned to her seat. "And please, my name is Elyssa."

"All right, then, Elyssa. Hungry or not, you will eat." He knew better, what with the way she eyeballed the meat when Hobbs brought in the tray. She was starved. She may be accustomed to forfeiting her meal portions in the company of men, but here on his ship, everyone received an equal share. Well, everyone but Rathbone.

Midway through the meal, Blackthorn's curiosity got the better of him. "For a woman mourning the death of her husband, I find it odd you have abandoned his name."

"I've accepted his death, but I have not abandoned his name. I am a Montgomery."

"Yes, yes, for the interest of your father." And he needn't be reminded of her station, either. He had already spent her ransom money he'd collect on a plot of land, or maybe a tavern, in Puerto Rico.

"If I am to be cooped up in the captain's quarters, with no one else to talk with, at least I can be addressed on familiar terms with him."

"Very well. But you will continue to address me as Captain." For no other reason than to remind her she was still under his command.

"Certainly." She returned her attention to her plate.

The remainder of their meal was taken in silence and the lass took great pains to avoid eye contact. He didn't mind. It gave him plenty of opportunity to admire his companion as she ate, focusing on her lips, her neck, her small wrists, her bosom. If she looked at him when she stood to refresh his cup, again, he didn't notice. He couldn't tear his eyes away from the view she presented as she bent to pour his rum.

"This is the third time you've topped off my mug, lass. It'll take a lot more than a flagon of rum for me to forget about my bath."

She offered a sheepish grin. "'Twas worth a try."

He chuckled. "Yes, I suppose it was. But alas, I left instruction with Mister Kipp to have a basin and warm rainwater brought to my cabin at the second dog watch."

As if on cue, the knell of the ship's bell tolled. Elyssa slowly set the flagon down, but did not release the handle. With the knock at the door, she filled her cup and gulped down the liquor.

Blackthorn laughed heartily.

"Enter."

Two deck hands carried in his bath water. Two more, the basin. All wore a smirk of envy while ogling the woman.

"Pay heed, boys. You're sloshing water on the floor."

As quick as they entered, they were gone. And not soon enough. He was more than ready for her hands to rub upon his body.

She poured another cup. Blackthorn put a hand to her wrist, stopping her from tossing it down her throat. "Pour the water in the basin, Elyssa." He took the mug from her and nodded to the buckets.

She took a deep breath, likely for courage. "Yes, Captain."

He leaned against the table and watched as she followed his orders. Giving commands had never been so fun.

"My boots." He uncrossed his ankles and lifted his foot.

She gave him an incredulous look before kneeling to remove his boots. She tugged and tugged again, falling back on her arse when his foot slipped free. He just smiled at her, giving her his other foot whilst she picked herself up off her backside. This time, she had been careful to keep her balance. Blackthorn removed his cutlass and crimson sash from his waist and shed his tunic. Any chill he may have felt from removing his shirt was quickly chased away with her heated gaze upon his chest. Her cheeks reddened once she realized he'd caught her staring. What a darling shade of rose. This game was far more enticing than he ever imagined. Oh, but he was a wicked man. Moral or not, he couldn't let this delectable moment pass him by.

"My trousers, little one. Unlace my trousers."

"Captain Blackthorn!" Her cheeks, and now her pretty little nose, turned bright red. "Please don't make me do this."

"Surely you've seen a man naked before."

"Well, yes. Er, no."

"Didn't you see your husband naked?"

"Um..."

"Didn't you?"

She blew out a frustrated sigh. "It was always dark."

Dark? Blessed be. What kind of man was this Dobie? Wouldn't he want to see her in the light? Blackthorn would bet his brace of pistols she'd be glorious in nothing but her flesh. Another thought crept in.

"You're not a—"

"Virgin? No, Captain. Just we hadn't many occasions to be intimate."

"How long were you married?"

"A fortnight before we set sail."

'Twas plenty of time to be intimate with a newly wed wife. This Dobie chap was a dolt.

"Certainly you must see what a flagrant position you have put me in. Are you married, Captain Blackthorn?"

Ah, trying to postpone the inevitable with useless prattle. "Circumstances of my occupation have kept me from the betrothal post." That and losing the woman he once loved to a wrongful accusation. All those promises of a wealth, status, and family flew away on a blustery wind after his discharge from the Royal Navy. He was innocent and she refused to stand by him. Staring down her nose at him, she turned him away and never looked back.

He was in no mood to blemish the evening with buried transgressions. "As long as you're staying in my cabin, you'll need to rid yourself of your modesty. You're bound to see me unclothed at some point."

"You are a rake, plain and true."

If she only knew how much her delightful, pouty scowl spurned him on. She was a spitfire under that propriety. He'd like to see more of that side of her. "My trousers, Elyssa."

She tipped her chin up and straightened her back. "Very well, Captain Blackthorn." Defiance leavened her tone. And he liked it.

She dove headlong into the task, deftly loosening the laces. Not breaking eye contact, she quipped, "Would you like for me to pull them off, too?"

"But of course."

Her nostrils flared and her jaw clenched. What sport to anger her. He was having a damned good time.

In one brisk swoop, Elyssa yanked his breeches down. She gasped as he sprang free, eye to eye, he was completely erect. And why not? He'd been aroused by her the moment she wrapped those sweet lips around her first forkful of meat and grew steadily stiff since.

Elyssa popped up, redder than a rose in full bloom.

"There now. 'Twasn't so terrible, was it?"

"'Twas worse." She rubbed her hands quickly up and down the front of her skirt in a fit of nerves.

He chuckled. "So you say, but I think you quite enjoy seeing me naked."

"Pardon me if I vehemently disagree."

She could disagree till the sea dried up, but he knew better. He saw the unmistakable glint of lust in her eyes. Granted it had been brief. All the same it was definitely there.

"Enough ogling, lass."

Her mouth fell open in disbelief.

"I'm ready for my bath."

She huffed, snatching up the rag she had used on herself the night before. He stepped into the shallow basin and sat down. The warm water relieved the stress cramped in his lower back. His muscles reminded him just how long ago his last relaxing bath had been. Since Kingston, with a voracious, bawdy doxy named Frannie. Blackthorn doubted Elyssa would show him the same unchaste ministrations as Frannie. Nevertheless, anticipation bubbled inside his chest as she knelt beside him and lathered a chip of soap in the wet rag.

He was a wicked man, for sure.

Elyssa made hasty work with the rough, knotty rag scrubbing him clean. She scoured over his shoulders and back with a little too much force. Any harder and she'd scourge his flesh right off. Scents of floral perfume assailed his nose. Criminy. The lass used the fragrant soap of the Frenchwoman. She'd have him smelling like a foppish milksop. Devilish girl.

She made her way around to his collarbone, rubbing him from his neck down. He relished the feel of her soft hands kneading into his muscles rougher than necessary. Damn, what would those hands feel like digging into his back as he took her. He'd best rid himself of lewd thoughts. *You can't sully the pawn, Bran.* He grunted at the thought.

She looked up and he held her in his gaze. Such a pretty face. For a moment, she paused. The heat from her hand seeped through the cloth. A mixture of innocence and temerity whirled within her eyes. He could wander around those brown beauties for hours. Why, he couldn't fathom. Must be because he hadn't been in port in two moons. Aye, he missed the touch of a woman, 'twas all.

Her eyelids flickered, a wee smile graced her sweet lips, and she resumed scrubbing, slower, without trying to peel away layers of skin.

Lathering up the rag again, the bar of soap slipped and plopped into the water. It came to a rest between his legs. Elyssa let out an adorable yip. Bless him, but this couldn't get any better. He raised an eyebrow at her expectantly. Dare she reach for it? She wouldn't, that he knew. But a man could wish.

Quite by surprise, her hand zipped into the water. Tremors raced across his inner thighs with the skim of her fingers. *Blimey!* His reaction to her brief touch startled him. Damn, he hadn't been *that* long without a woman's touch.

Poor chit. He didn't think it possible she could turn redder, but she did.

He smirked. "I could have gotten that for you."

She smacked the rag to his chest. Soapy water splattered into his face. "Not without suggestive quibble." She returned to scrubbing his flesh.

"By the way you bite your bottom lip when you look at me, I'd say you are not offended in the least. I'd say you are as attracted to me as I am to you."

"I don't know what you are talking about." She stroked the cloth over his chest, the rag scraping over his nipples. With her free hand, she rubbed the lather in circles. He daresay the lass was enjoying herself. The devil knows Blackthorn was. Her slippery fingers gliding over his torso and down his abdomen drove him mad.

Never once did she venture below the water line. Didn't matter. The lass had already bewitched him.

He cupped her chin and seized her lips. Branding her, pressing into her mouth. Elyssa didn't recoil. No, instead she returned his kiss. For that, he lingered. By thunder what the hell had come over him? Reluctantly, he released her. She tilted her head away, making a go of chewing her lip off.

"Aye. You cannot deny it." He grabbed her chin again and forced her to look at him. "You cannot deny me." Clouds of desire in her gaze were blown away with the drop of his last word.

"Deny you, I will." She slapped away his hand. "You'd have me weak and take advantage of my position."

"I've no use for a feeble poppet. And you, dear girl, are not weak." Anger crept from the crevices of his good temper. She'd made him hard as a shipboard's iron cannon with her coy smile and deft hands. And, by saints, her mouth! "I've yet to take what is rightfully mine under the circumstances." *My bollocks are about to pop off and she claims I'm taking advantage of her. Bah!* "But I think I'll start now."

Blackthorn grabbed the back of her head and crushed his mouth to hers. She struggled, fought for purchase by pushing against his chest. Her wet hands simply slipped off. Stings to his flesh as she slapped his shoulders and face did nothing to dull the ire and passion surging through him. He mauled and fed upon her delicious lips. Only when she ceased fighting him did the fire within him cool to a simmer.

He wasn't done. Not yet. Her threaded his hand in her hair and gently yanked her head back, exposing the creamy pillar of her neck. He latched on with one lascivious kiss. So soft, so savory.

A hushed cry broke his randy haze.

He growled into her flesh. "What have you done?" He wasn't sure if he spoke to her or to himself.

His grip on her hair loosened and she fell away. Fear and hurt registered across her visage, even as she licked her lips.

Anger domineered his mind. Not at the lass, but at himself. He slipped down below the water. He'd never forced a woman to kiss him before. Throes of passion were one thing, but handling her roughly was inexcusable. 'Twas her fault. He lost himself. He must regain control.

Taking the soap, he finished bathing, scrubbing in all the places she wouldn't dare go, cleansing his hair and body as if he could wash away the last few moments. He stood and stepped out of the basin, not caring about decency in her presence. Water fled from his body in torrents, leaving puddles in his wake as he crossed the floor to retrieve a towel from his locker.

Elyssa, eyes downcast whilst he tugged on his breeches, stood on the opposite side of the cabin. Chewing her bottom lip. What did that mean? Damn but if he couldn't read her. She cast some kind of spell upon him. He wanted her. He wanted her badly, and he couldn't trust himself around her. He couldn't chance tainting a ransom for her. A man of Samuel Montgomery's status would not have a defiled girl mar his good name. He'd cast her out giving no claim or wealth on her behalf.

Hell's fury, if she wasn't worth the chance.

He had to remind himself she'd just lost her husband. Why did he think she'd readily receive him? Because he was more of a man than her late dolt of a husband. Nay—he couldn't let jealous, unfounded reasoning muddle his mind.

"I won't apologize, not for kissing you."

"Nor will I."

Puzzled, he asked, "For?"

She pointed to his neck. "Scratching you."

Blackthorn reached up and felt the slashes on his throat made by her fingernails. He hadn't noticed them before, but now the gashes stung.

He smirked, decidedly liking the burn. A war wound in a battle hinged in an uneasy truce. In three strides, he stood a breath away from her. He put a finger to her chin and tipped her face up to meet his stare. "You'd do well not to deny me."

"Threaten and punish me as you see fit, Captain Blackthorn." She spoke as if merely imparting facts. No malice, no fear. As if the conversation was over a spot of tea. "I will grant you all you desire but those of the flesh. Not without a fight."

Oh, what a conquest the lass would be. Should he pursue the quarry. Which he would not. Bewitching as she was. With her magical hands, her heaving bosom, her parted, swollen lips. *Shit!* No, he could not trust himself around her.

"Duly noted." He didn't bother with the laces of his trousers. He needed to get away. Now. He scooped up his tunic and retreated.

CHAPTER 5

Elyssa set aside yet another mended pair of breeches and stretched her cramped fingers. Seems the men on this ship were in a desperate need of a haberdasher. Their clothing was threadbare at best. She didn't mind the task. Sewing kept her busy. Being busy kept her from thinking about *him*.

If she hadn't lost all sense of time, it'd been four days since Captain Blackthorn had left her in a state of wanton decadence. She had cursed him for it, too, and cursed herself for not being as offended or disgusted by his indecency. Quite the contrary. To see him in his glory, by God, she should be struck down, for he was magnificent. Elyssa was beside herself, not knowing how to handle bathing a formidable, dangerous pirate. She pretended desperately not to focus on the planes and ripples of his muscles under her hands, how smooth and divine he felt. Did he notice she had become distracted, not scrubbing but stroking his taut body instead?

And his kiss! His kiss alone melted her insides. Never had she been kissed with such passion. She was completely governable, unable to make one coherent thought. Not until he spoke of denial and bullied her with threats. If there was anything she'd learned since becoming a seaman, it was not to let anyone bully her. The weak were targets for trouble. A man must hold his own and prove himself, lest he become a victim of cruel torment. Elyssa did her best balancing inconspicuousness and fortitude among the *Maraville* men. Even in the face of consequence, she would do the same with the captain.

But, heavens, that second kiss. Of course she fought him. What else could she have done? He damn near attacked her. At first, she had been frightened. Afraid he would violate her. It didn't take her long to understand just how possessive his rough kiss had been. At least that had been what she thought. Now she wasn't so sure.

Four days.

He hadn't been back in his cabin at all. She wished he'd return—if only for another bath. She may well perish waiting. Nay, she was weary of waiting. She'd see the captain one way or another.

A knock at the door drew her from visions of a naked, libidinous pirate.

"Afternoon, Mrs. Montgomery."

"Good afternoon, Mister Kipp."

Mister Kipp had been her only human contact since the captain left her to wither away. No longer embarrassed around the first mate, Kipp proved to be quite the conversationalist. He was rough around the edges, but he told fascinating stories and wonderful jokes.

Kipp dropped an armload of woolen stockings at her feet. "More mendin'," he said.

"Criminy, Kipp. Why don't you fellows chase down a merchant ship with clothing? You're pirates, for pity's sake." She winked at him.

"Ain't nothin' out here but a bunch of Frenchies. The boys would rather have their toenails ripped off 'fore they dress like a fop."

"You're terrible." She giggled.

"Aye. That I be."

"Kipp, will you do me a favor?"

"Now, lass. You know I can't talk to ya 'bout where we're goin'. And I already got a tongue lashin' from the capt'n fer speakin' to yer friend, Mac."

"I know. I'm sorry for that. But, it's just—" Elyssa couldn't believe what she was about to ask. Being cooped up in this cabin had made her delirious. "I'd like to speak with the captain."

"Not sure he be wantin' to see ya, lass."

She had inquired more than once about Captain Blackthorn. Kipp remained tight-lipped, saying 'twasn't his place to discuss the captain in personal matters. He did let it slip that the captain had been unusually cross-tempered, snapping at his crew like a termagant old maid.

"I understand." Well, no, she didn't understand. She didn't have any idea why he had shunned her like an infectious plague. "He might be interested to know about his log book."

"Oh no, Mrs. Montgomery, you didn't." Kipp grimaced, his brow crimped in worry. He locked his hands behind his neck and shook his head. "By God, lass, what were ya thinkin'?"

Elyssa's stomach suddenly churned with her salted pork breakfast and a lump of sickness that she had made a terrible mistake. She pressed on regardless, passing a glance to the chamber pot. "I think he'll be pleased with what I found."

"Why don't I just forget ya told me this," Kipp said. "Aye, ya said nothin' 'bout the Capt'n's books."

She needed him to deliver the message before she changed her mind. "Please, Kipp. Just tell him I wish to discuss his ledger."

"I warn ya, lass. He'll be hoppin' mad. I'd keep the table between you and him, I would."

"Thank you, sir."

'Twas good advice. Elyssa planted herself behind the desk and anxiously waited for Captain Blackthorn. The minutes ticked off. She was beginning to think Kipp didn't relay the message.

She had sunk into his chair just as the door crashed open. Elyssa couldn't get to her feet fast enough and banged her knee against the table.

"You are a brave little chit." He spat out the words and kicked the door shut. Malice roiled from him, filling the room thick enough she could breathe it.

"I—"

"If not stupid."

He towered at the edge of the desk, stalking around to reach her. She distanced herself by moving around the table with each step he took. "But—"

"Cross me, will you?"

"No." Thank God for the desk. If she survived Captain Blackthorn's wrath, she would thank Kipp for the solid counsel. "Listen—

"I will not listen to a no-good, prying bit of fluff."

Prying? Bit of fluff? How dare he! Anger flushed over her. "What would you have me do, Captain? You've left me to my own devices in here for four days. Four days!"

"You've no right nosing in my desk."

"I'd been searching for paper to write my father a letter. Humph. And you thought I'd sit here like a good little girl and mend stockings all day? Maybe you are the stupid one." *Uh-oh.* The words tumbled out before she could stop herself.

He was too fast. In a blink, he had her by her arms. His fingers dug deep. Fire burned in his darkening eyes. "A spiteful tongue can be removed."

"You're hurting me."

The curl of his lip twitched, his frown unfastened one stitch. Though his grip slackened, he did not let her go. She took the brief respite to her favor.

"I'm not used to spending so much time alone. And though it is a paltry excuse, my curiosity got the better of me."

"Which has gotten you into dire straits."

"Please. If you'd just let me show you what I've found."

"Why would I do that?"

"Because you are terrible at arithmetic."

His grip tightened once again and he pulled her close to his scowling face. "First you trespass upon me, then you pry into my business, and now you are insulting me. I'll not suffer a moment more from the likes of you."

"Best I point out this flaw now so as to protect your profits later. You are also miscalculating your cargo's worth. And the men you're doing business with know it."

His pupils widened as his gaze bore into hers. She hadn't meant to goad the beast. But she didn't entirely regret it. She should be fearful of him. Instead, his ire, his harsh handling excited her. Reckless, that was what she was.

"If you release me, I can show you how much more profit you can make on the cargo in your hold."

He tilted his head suspiciously. "Why would I believe this?"

"You forget I am a shipper's daughter. I managed my father's books for years. And I can double your revenue."

"Is that so?"

That got his attention. He let go of one arm, but kept his grip tight on the other. She suspected he would not let her forget who controlled her. Pulling her back behind the desk, he forced her to sit. The captain opened a drawer, retrieved his logbook, and flipped to the page of his last entries.

"Show me."

Elyssa explained that the cost of some goods had increased, in part due to the rise in cargos being lost to pirates. His pert chuckle to her statement died within the irony. He'd been away from port long enough his figures were not accurate with the rapidly changing market. The captain bent over her shoulder to get a better look at the book. His breath landed upon her shoulder sending warm chills along her neck, down to her breasts, and beyond. Her head spun with his musky scent. She willed herself to concentrate on her finger sliding down the crisp page of his logbook.

She pointed out the mathematical mistake he had made when logging in the cargo pilfered from the *Maraville*. By correcting it, he could earn a sizably larger profit in trade. Captain Blackthorn mumbled something under his breath about making the mistake when a pair of popinjays tussled outside his door. She cut her eyes over in time to catch the smirk flit across his handsome profile.

"Might I suggest aggrandizing your goods by rivaling merchants against one another?"

His eyebrows hitched up, clearly amused by her. "Now you are telling me how to run my affairs? I am no idiot, lass."

"Ahem, yes, well, I didn't mean to suggest you were."

His mouth, framed in days old stubble, coiled into a smile.

"By looking back at your past transactions" –*stop staring at his lips. You'll invite trouble*— "I see you had opportunities to increase your gains." *Trouble isn't all bad.* "If you take full advantage of the fluctuating market, you can manipulate merchants into paying you thrice the amount offered so as to keep ahead of competitors."

"Manipulate, you say."

The rise in his cheeks made Captain Blackthorn appear as if he were devising diabolical plans. She had an uneasy feeling those plans involved her.

"It isn't as intrepid as a pirate's occupation," she continued, "but take in consideration the time and labor it takes to plunder. It costs you money to sail, maintain a seaworthy ship, feed your men, and pay their labor. Gunpowder and shot are not cheap, either."

Husky laughter bounced off the cabin walls. He pushed off the back of her chair and sat on the edge of his desk facing her. "If I didn't know better, I'd say you were cut from the scarlet cloth of a pirate."

"I'm no pirate. I'm a bookkeeper."

"You use means to exploit with numbers. I exploit using fear and open gun ports." He crossed his arms over the expanse of his chest. "There's not much difference between us."

Elyssa hadn't thought of it that way before. Was she really a thief? "It's simply business, nothing underhanded about it," she said, more to convince herself than the captain.

"This is true. Just as pirating is a business."

"But what I do is lawful."

"At times, what I do is as well. Is it lawful to milk patrons? I'd think not."

"'Tis only an opinion."

"A sound one. Never mind that. You intrigue me, Elyssa. Loyal daughter, beautiful widow, spirited seaman, and intelligent bookkeeper. You're something of an enigma."

Beautiful? There he goes again, commenting on beauty. Come now, Elyssa. Keep your head. He mentioned you were intelligent, too. Give him a taste of how intelligent you are. "I'd like to introduce a proposition."

"Bold of you."

Could he be any smugger? "Release me as your valet and I shall help you with your books."

"No."

"No?"

"No. I quite enjoy the idea of you serving me. Shamefully, I have not used you enough. I fully mean to rectify that."

Her heart sank. The despicable man. He meant to make her miserable.

"Instead of mending clothes or doing other menial chores, you will show me your bookkeeping knowledge. Understand I will still require you to see to my needs. Start servicing me now."

"Do you require another bath?" *Oh, my.* When did she turn brazen?

"Anxious to finish the job, are you?"

Heat flushed her face. "If I'm to be in close proximity with you, I'd prefer you not smell like fish bait."

He bent down, grabbing the arms of the chair, and pinned her to her seat. "Do I smell like fish bait, little one? If not, I could wallow in the hull's bilge water."

Elyssa relished the captain's levity and mischievous smile. She longed to keep him in good humor. It didn't matter what he had her do as long as she was near him. This revelation startled her.

The captain laughed, a glorious sound. "Best you start with filling my cup with rum, before you chew off your bottom lip."

He pushed off the chair to give her room to rise. In an instant, she regretted not bantering further with him. Perhaps if she had she would still be nose to nose with him.

"Then we will take a closer look at my…log."

The last few days had Elyssa floating on a wondrous cloud. She had looked forward to the day's work with Captain Blackthorn. Despite what he claimed otherwise, the captain's arithmetic sorely lacked. Together they had uncovered several more mistakes and she had adjusted his numbers to better suit him when he sold his cargo. He had taken his supper with her each evening, as well as engaging in idle chatter. Having his attention, sharing her knowledge of sturdier financial affairs with him, soaking in his heat, his musk, his throaty laugh, made her twittery with expectation of seeing him again.

But they had finished his books. He had no reason to come to her today. Many excuses to call for him bounded through her mind. She'd considered "finding" another mathematical error. In the end, she knew she'd appear transparent in wanting his company. Her fingers ached from chewing the skin around her nails bare, wondering when she'd see him.

What a scandalous way to be in, pining for a pirate, the keeper of her shackles. Yet she couldn't help but fall into his eyes when he looked upon her. *Moon-eyed goosecap.*

A quick rap on the door and Captain Blackthorn flourished into the cabin. Giggles of relief bubbled forth.

Blackthorn had no good reason for dining with Elyssa, other than it pleased him. So few things pleased him these days. A fine bottle of wine, a silver-laden quarry, an occasional night of lusty sin, pleased him, to be sure. But the sense of fulfillment was fleeting. Shame, really. His thirst for the bounty of pirating had ceased to sate him some time ago. Now the only thing he thirsted for was the bonny lass stealing coy glances at him over the rim of her cup.

She'd invaded his every waking moment. Her heavenly smile, the faintest hint of perfumed skin, the tiny hitch in her breath when he drew too near. Even their conversations he replayed in his mind. He'd been most curious about her dreams to run her own shipping business. What an audacious venture. One which made her all the most admirable. More than once, he stole peeks down her tunic as he leaned over her shoulder, pretending to scrutinize his log books. He had been scrutinizing, all right. Scrutinizing how her breasts would feel in the palm of his hand. Scrutinizing the taste of her flesh as he dragged his tongue down the valley of her chest to her most coveted spot. If he were honest with himself, he was happy with her prancing through his thoughts, rollicking in visions of naked limbs and crumbled sheets. Gave him something else to languish upon rather than the uncertainty of another wasted day. Damned pity to have taken a liking to her. Once he ransomed her off, he'd be back to his roving. At least until he got word from Christensen.

The sooner, the better. There was no room for an angel in his life. And a pirate's ship was no place for a woman. They could be attacked by the Royal Navy at any time. Aye, he needed to get rid of her.

But tonight, he would enjoy her until his plundering instincts fired up.

"I'm curious, Captain Blackthorn." Elyssa removed his empty dinner plate and stacked it with her own. "And please," she said. "I do not mean to step from politeness nor disparage you." She topped off his mug with a fresh bottle of liquor. "Why have you chosen your trade?"

Her question took him aback. It was unsuitable conversation between the likes of him and a woman. "'Tis not a story for a lady's ears."

"I don't doubt that. But it is one I want to hear. You know about me, and yet, I know little of you."

He leaned back in his chair, slowly rubbing the prickly stubble of his chin. No doxy had ever wanted to know him as a man, or why he was a pirate. Seemed those strumpets were simply excited to be bedded by a dangerous rogue, thrilled he would shower them with his ill-gotten gold for a swive.

She had no idea how vexing her request was, or how much he wanted to lay the most beautiful jeweled necklace upon her throat. No ill-gotten gold coins for her. Why he felt that way about this bit of fluff was beyond him. 'Twas like trying to make out a shape in the shadows of night. He just couldn't quite form the answer. "I'm just another man lawful society condemned."

"What was your crime?" She rested her chin into her palm with genuine curiosity.

"'Tis unimportant." He truly wished it were so.

"I believe it to be quite important, as turning pirate guarantees a hanging at low tide."

He chuckled. "I bow my head to the executioner who pulls the lever and leaves me kicking the wind."

"You trifle with big talk."

Despair, swilled with anger, clouded his mind. "Do not make a mistake, lass. I am deserving of the devil's scourge. From the very moment I spilled innocent blood, my sins thereafter were of little consequence. No holy cleansing, no absolution would ever rectify what had been done."

"Innocent?"

"A boy, dead, by my hand." He glared at her, wanting to put fear into her. She should not forget he was a pirate in every sense of the word. Her life was at his discretion.

"You killed a boy?" Her eyes grew the size of doubloons. "How?"

"You're an intrusive chit."

"Perhaps. But if you wish to frighten me, to which you are trying so hard to do, then you should tell me what darkness led you to become a cruel, vicious man, which incidentally, you are not."

"You make a grave mistake to misjudge me."

"Then prove to me I am wrong. Tell me what happened."

He would rather talk more about her, hear more stories of the little girl who once sneaked into her papa's office and scribbled pictures of flowers and kittens in all his record books, of how she preferred riding her mare in the rain to prattling with genteel ladies over tea, and of the dreams she had not so long ago of running a business of her own.

Blackthorn crossed his arms over his chest. Elyssa wasn't going to let the conversation die. Much like the ghosts of his past still haunting him. If she wanted to know what kind of monster he was, then he would tell her. Mayhap her disgust and fear in him would make it all the more easier to rid himself of her in New Providence.

"He was my charge while docked in Antigua. The sixteen year-old son of Admiral Drummond of the Royal Navy. The upstart let no one forget it, always using threats of castigation or removal if he didn't get his way." No one had wanted to challenge the lad, or go up against his equally arrogant father. Blackthorn didn't have a problem with putting the boy in his place, and he wasn't scared of Admiral Drummond, either. He supposed that was one reason why Joseph had been assigned to him. The other reason was what got him killed.

"He demanded to be taught swordplay, specifically without the pleasantries of prescribed behavior. But the little shit had no discipline." Elyssa was unaffected by his vulgar tongue. Instead, she listened intently, her hands cupped tightly around her mug. Criminy, the lass had been around crude jack tars too long.

Blackthorn remembered well Joseph's barbing slurs on his bastardized breeding, contemptuous eye rolling and sneers. Many occasions had Blackthorn tempering his urge to backhand the sprat.

The day the boy met his death had been no different.

He had taken Joseph up to a grassy bluff overlooking the craggy shoreline of English Harbour for lessons. Wind swept up the cliff in blustery bursts. The air was heavy and smelled of a recent rain. Blackthorn had been out of sorts, hearing a rumor his betrothed was seen without an escort in a garden with another man. He'd been in no mood for Joseph's backbiting.

"He adopted a terrible technique, overextending himself in thrusts. Forevermore I had to correct him, until I began kicking his legs from under him each time he left his flank exposed. The boy didn't appreciate kissing the ground time and again. He took to name-calling and threatening me. I ordered him to hold his clack, to stand down." Joseph had been wild-eyed, his mouth twitched with hate. Blackthorn should have known he was foolish enough to not obey.

"He attacked. I disarmed him easily enough, and with the tip of my blade tucked neatly under his chin, I informed him I would no longer be his teacher. He promised to have me imprisoned for dereliction." One of the greatest moments of Blackthorn's miserable life was the dumbfounded look on Joseph's pompous mug when he told the bastard to flog off.

Joseph had sworn Blackthorn would regret his mistake. He'd been right.

"I walked away. The boy went into a fit of anger, retrieved his weapon from the ground, and charged me. When I spun around, he impaled upon my sword." Elyssa's tiny gasp did not compare to the one that escaped from Joseph's lips. The shock, the fear in Joseph's eyes, burned a hellish hole into Blackthorn's soul. As much as he hated the princock, he hadn't wanted him dead.

Blackthorn threw back the rest of his nearly full mug of rum. The bitter liquor scalded down his throat. No amount of the elixir would wash away the boy's blood tainting his existence.

"I removed my blade and he stumbled backward,"—tears and blood had flowed freely— "falling off the cliff to the rocks below. Thus my fate was sealed."

"But it wasn't your fault."

"He was my responsibility."

"Surely you couldn't be blamed."

"I was. And I was stripped of my honor and my occupation." Apparently he should have been more fearful of Joseph's father, or rather, what the Admiral could do. "Admiral Drummond had me imprisoned for murder. I was to be hung, but I managed an escape." Blackthorn would never forget how Christensen risked his own life to slip him a key. He gave Blackthorn a fighting chance, nothing more. Blackthorn hoped to return the favor someday.

"So you turned to piracy?"

"What better way to live a condemned life than to turn on the country who would throw me out like the filth mucking a chamber pot. To plunder English merchants and wreak havoc to British trade."

"But why did you attack the *Maraville*?"

He shrugged. "I just don't care for Spaniards."

"So you've gone to war with all of mankind."

"'Twas the only trade I could pick up a living. A mighty fine one, at that. Losing it all, now I take what I may, including you." He lifted his empty mug and she quickly saw to her duty. Good. He had reacquainted her with her precarious position as a pirate's captive. "Tell me, chit. What do you think of me now?"

"I don't see an evil rogue. I see a wounded man. Forced to this life by circumstance, and not accepting the unjust opinions condemning him."

What? He didn't understand. Why wasn't she quaking in her boots? She should be, no, *needed* to be fearful of him. "I kill for my own gain."

Her eyes wandered over him, caressing him like the exotic silks of the Far East. She smiled. "I have a feeling you don't kill unless the screws are put to you. Nay, you would rather coerce your quarries with intimidation."

"What leads you to believe such drivel?"

"Captain Alonso engaged you, and yet no one was killed in battle. You let us—them—all live, knowing once they reach port, Alonso would speak of your atrocity, knowing his story will spread fear that you prey in these waters."

'Twas true. All of it. Damn her. An odd sense of relief buoyed him. She understood him. He'd said nothing to defend himself. He hadn't tried to make her feel his pain. And yet, the lass saw through him. He hadn't meant for her to sympathize with him. What the bloody hell had he been thinking? Telling her his story came to naught. He'd been less surprised had his flintlock exploded in his face.

Well, he'd rectify that now. For his own sake.

He grabbed her wrist as she tried to return to her seat. "You *will* fear me, little one."

CHAPTER 6

"Oh I do, Captain Blackthorn. I fear you will not kiss me again."

Whatever was in the rum must have gone to her head. She was more surprised by her words than the captain. With the trouble she invited, she needed more of the poison. How inappropriate would it be if she drank straight from bottle she held?

Inappropriate. Confound it. She should be appalled by her improper behavior. Just what was the appropriate way she should act around a dashing pirate captain with enchanting fallow eyes? 'Twas madness. Of course, it could have been the Captain's touch, warm and calloused, behind her loose talk. He held her firm and possessive. Much like the crocodile smile he wore.

"Do you *want* me to kiss you?"

Rum. Rum. Should I drink more rum? Would he be angry if she emptied the bottle? "It would be imprudent to expect as such from you."

"And if I do kiss you?"

"I will have taken what I want from you—vilifying you. But you are not the contemptible man you want me to believe you to be."

In a move so fast, the room spun in a blur, he twirled her around and planted her onto his lap. She yipped, dropping the bottle on the floor. The rum gurgled out, spreading an amber pool onto the worn wooden floor. Her hands splayed across his expansive chest. She labored to control her rapid breathing, to swallow down the heartbeat pulsing in her throat. Lord help her for she had fallen into his eyes, ablaze with fire and hunger. And he was about to devour her. *Hurry, please.*

He seized her mouth, ravaging, pillaging, delving deep with his tongue. His brandied taste drove her to take him in kind. Boldly she explored his mouth. Wild, undisciplined, wanton, she cared not. She was awash in his passion.

He held her firm by the crook of her hip. But he needn't worry with holding her still. There was no other place in the world she'd rather be than in his embrace. His other hand slid up her waist, rounding under the crimped lace lining her bodice to cup her breast. The rough pad of his thumb rubbed across the tender pucker of her nipple. Shards of tingles shot pleasure straight to her crux.

Elyssa swallowed much needed air when his lips left hers. Before she could protest, he tugged her bodice lower and captured her breast. She moaned and arched her back, giving him more of her bosom. He seemed obliged as he groped and tweaked her other breast. The hard planes of his chest gave way to the rise of his shoulder. Grateful to be able to feel his taut back again, she explored every inch of him she could reach. She badly wished to remove his tunic. Worthless piece of cloth was in the way.

A chill cooled her damp chest. Blackthorn had abandoned her nipples for the dip of her throat, suckling, kissing, and making his way up to her jaw. By God. How could devilish kisses along her jaw be so pure? Nothing could be more sensual. Until he reached her earlobe. His wet mouth landing upon her ear had been enough to cause surrender. But the invasion of his playful tongue was a downright dirty trick. Her flesh had come alive. She shivered with the thrill skittering down her arms and across the tips of her nipples. What wonders this man did to her body.

The captain's nimble hand had the hem of her skirt bunched up to her lap. He made long strokes up and down her thigh. A whole new sensation rapidly roared to life. Squeezing her knees together served to make the throbbing worse between her legs.

"How far can I go before you fear me, Elyssa?" His hot breath fanning in her ear sent a fresh wave of ripples all the way down to her toes. "How far?"

Lost in a feverish haze, she wanted him to take her as far as the endless sea would go. She could think of nothing more. 'Twas impossible to think beyond that very moment.

"I will not…fear you, Captain…Blackthorn."

"Bran." He dragged his tongue down her neck and back up to her ear. "Call me Bran."

"Bran." She wasn't in so much of a fog that she didn't realize the implication of using his given name. 'Twas a stout name, deservingly so, and she liked the power it gave her to say it. "Take me as far as you dare."

He growled into her neck, searing her with another wicked kiss. "Don't tempt me, lass."

"But I must."

Bran leaned back to stare into her eyes, no doubt gauging his next move by her reaction. Was she foolish to dare him? Perhaps. No matter, she offered him an impish pout anyhow. He swooped her up into his arms, kicked his chair away, and planted her on the edge of the table.

"I'll be a gentleman no more." He shoved her skirt up around her waist. The smooth wood of the table was cold against her bare bum. With her naked breasts and her exposed juncture, she felt enlivened, primed.

He wedged himself between her legs. Elyssa frantically removed his shirt tucked beneath his trousers. No sooner had he shed the damned thing, she stroked his defined muscles. She hadn't realized how much she missed feeling them. Her terribly marred hands born of the seaman's trade seemed unnaturally pale against his bronzed skin. The contrast was not much different from pairing a widowed bookkeeper and a disgraced pirate.

Making quick work of his breeches, he attacked her again with an open mouth. She readily received him, more anxious, she thought, than he.

Bran rubbed his hand across her sheath, petting her folds. She whimpered into his kiss. Back and forth he caressed, drawing his middle finger over her throbbing nub. With each pass the pressure built. She broke from his kiss and threw her head back. Glory be! She had never felt such abandoned pleasure. Never knew it existed. Just when she thought she could take no more, he stopped. She whimpered again.

Elyssa opened her eyes and was startled. Brown eyes boring into her exemplified his intent and decisive execution. She flinched upon the tip of his shaft touching her aching folds. Slowly, he eased into her, pushing in all the way, allowing her to adjust to his girth without causing too much pain.

"You're tight, little one. Relax. I won't hurt you." His voice poured over her like molasses, sweet and thick. He lulled her with his avow and he leaned in to repeat his instruction. "Relax."

His hands rounded to her buttocks and he scooted her to the very edge of the desk, lancing her upon him further. She squealed, or moaned, she wasn't sure which. But the stab of pleasure sent her reeling for more. Elyssa buried her face into his neck, an adequate spot for refuge. Bran pulled completely out only to slide back in, three, maybe four more times. 'Twas a vicious torment. She needed him to fill her, stay within her, to join together with her.

"Please, Bran."

A low chuckle rumbled from his throat. "You are a bewitching treat, my dear. Bewitching and impossible to resist."

Obliging her, he guided in, pushing to his hilt. He measured a steady pace, rocking into her. Her fingers dug into his arms and she strove to meet him thrust for thrust. His skin had become damp from her hurried breathing. Unfettered urges inspired her to kiss and feed upon his neck. Mother of Heaven she could not get enough of this man.

She would not be remorseful later of what she wanted so badly now. But then she was drunk, drunk on his possessive mouth, briny musk and searing touch. The drunk were impaired, fluid, careless. Never mind, she would bear the circumstance later. For now, she would drink her fill of Captain Bran Blackthorn.

Eddies of vibrating bliss swirled tighter, quicker with his rhythm. Higher and higher she rose, faster and faster he pumped. All the while, he feasted upon her exposed shoulder and tangling his hand into her hair. Damn, but he made her dizzy. Her fingernails gouged into his arms, asserting what was left of her meager thread of control to something tangible. Suddenly her spinning bliss exploded. She seized, unable to cry out, unable to unwrap her legs that had somehow wrapped themselves around Bran's waist. Lights and shadows surged on wave after wave of quivering pleasure.

Bran continued to pump, slamming into her until he, too, stiffened upon his release.

In that moment, locked with him in salacious sin, Elyssa had fallen. Fallen from what, she dared not entertain. But she had a suspicion.

Her short married life had been void of carnal pleasures. A quick shag to ease Dobie's desire was the most she received from her late husband. Had Dobie not perished from his fall, she would have never known what true indulgence of the flesh could be. She would have been trapped in a flaccid marriage. Elyssa shivered at the thought.

Bran kissed her again. This time, his lips were tender, not greedy. His eyes matched the affection he showed in one last peck, and then he withdrew. "I warned you not to tempt me."

"The only thing I regret is the splinter poking me in my arse."

That brought a crooked smile to his attractive mug.

"Besides," she added, "I told you I would not fear you."

A commotion clouded his expression. He warred with himself, or some thought, as he scanned her face, settling on her mouth. She bit her lip with a sudden flood of anxiety. Did he regret what he did, what *they* did? The humid heat between them lingered as he weighed her words.

"We are sailing into unfriendly waters." Bran pulled up her bodice, covering her breasts. He gave her his back and redressed. "There is a mighty fine chance the *Sanctum* will run into trouble. To ensure your safety, be ready to take orders."

Elyssa could not stop the deflating of her heart. To hell with any lurking danger out there. Her captain had turned cold. Their lovemaking didn't mean anything more to him than a dirty strum. *What did you expect, Elyssa? That he would shower you with flowers and bounty? Be grateful. To have him was what you wanted.* Still, she couldn't help the hurt and disappointment, or the sick feeling churning in the pit of her stomach.

"Bran." He glanced away from tying his sword into his sash to acknowledge he was listening. "You never said. What are you going to do with me?" 'Twas obvious he did not intend to keep her around as his woman. She couldn't dwell on that. What she needed was to know her fate now that her world had been forever changed.

"One thing you should know about pirates, love, we never reveal our course."

"Have mercy." She hoped begging would keep him from leaving her with unanswered questions and unrequited love. But he had already flung the door wide open.

"Remember, Mrs. Montgomery, I'm not the merciful type."

My God, man. You've done it again.

"You." Blackthorn grabbed the sleeve of a passing crewman. "Find Hobbs. Have him bring me a flagon of Hangman's Rum. Handsomely, now!"

Losing yourself with her. You're a bloody fool. But he cherished every moment with Elyssa. Every breath she took, every sound she made, her tightness around his cock, the way she released her modesty. Damn, he'd almost come undone the moment she spoke his name.

She was an angel. An angel he sullied. An angel he was to spend like sullied coin in a dangerous bargain.

Shit! He slammed his fist into the sloop's main mast. Pain shot through his white knuckles. He deserved far worse.

That fellow, Mac, Elyssa's friend, stared at him from across the cargo hold. The lad had taken to giving him a critical eye as of late. This but provoked Blackthorn, and he was feeling a mite confrontational.

"You got something to say, mate?"

Mac bowed his head in respect. "No, Capt'n."

"Aye. You do. You've got a grievance with me." The mackie wasn't getting off that easy. "Let's have it."

Mac lifted his chin, looking him dead in the eyes. "Just that Elysen, he—she—was a hard worker. Quick to learn her trade and never once complainin'. 'Twouldn't be just to do her harm." Mac's nostrils flared with the deep breath he took. "And, I'm wonderin' if you're an honorable man."

Hell no, he wasn't honorable. If he were, we wouldn't have taken Elyssa on his desk. He didn't have the decency to walk the extra steps to lay her on his bed. He was a bastard, right enough.

"You're a reckless one to not hold your clack."

Mac swallowed hard, but Blackthorn respected the paddy for not backing down.

"Don't worry over the likes of Mrs. Montgomery. She's fine." With that, Blackthorn gestured for Mac to take his leave.

"Hobbs says yer callin' for the Hangman." Kipp strolled up beside Blackthorn and handed him a bottle. "What's yer trouble?"

Blackthorn yanked out the cork with his teeth and spat it to the planks. "I tainted the pawn." He took a long quaff of the potent liquor. Spice and spirit singed his taste and washed down his gullet.

"Ain't surprised. You've been up in the sails over her."

"Hardly that."

Blackthorn walked to the rail. The horizon had disappeared into the veil of night. Black water below swallowed bits of flame cast by the ship's lone lantern hanging nearby. Nothing was visible of the sea beyond the fleeting light. He felt much the same way about his despicable soul and Elyssa—a fleeting light in a shrouded abyss.

"I've sailed with you for some five years now, Bran." Kipp clapped him on his shoulder. "I ain't never seen ya with that stupid grin on yer ugly mug. Every evenin' after leavin' her."

"Pish! No more of that scupper talk. I've tarnished the chances of a pardon, Kipp." He passed his first mate the bottle.

"A woman like that is worth a thousand hangin's."

Blackthorn couldn't agree more.

"The way I see it, brother, ain't much changed. No one on this boat knows who she is. No one has to know, either. 'Twas as it was before we took that Spanish merchant."

Kipp was right. The objective had been and still was the same—get the *Sanctum* a reprieve. Now it was to quietly make contact with Samuel Montgomery's officer and use a ransom for Elyssa as leverage. That should put the squeeze on Flynn.

Blackthorn nodded, pleased he still had control of the situation. "The sooner we reach Parlay Atoll, the better."

"We'll be droppin' anchor by the forenoon bell."

"Excellent. See that we pass New Providence's garrison with our colors flying."

"Ho, ho! You're a bold barracuda. You sure you haven't gone loose in the hilts with too much Hangman's Blood?"

"I find it a courtesy to Flynn to announce my arrival."

CHAPTER 7

The rabble in The Drowning Cup was much like the drinking holes Blackthorn had frequented in Port Royal. Marauders, strumpets, and thieves prowled in the shadows and crevices of the dark tavern. The air choked with tobacco, sweat, and stale ale. On a small dais in the back, a fiddler played. Two wenches, dressed in flashy feathers and beads and not much else, danced for the farthings tossed at their feet. And drunkards, plenty of drunkards, sat on every stool, at every table, carousing, singing, arguing, and gambling. Aye, The Drowning Cup was a fine establishment for wayward jack tars, rogue wreckers, and scavengers. And a great place to push aside fanciful thoughts of a certain doe-eyed angel.

Blackthorn found it ironic the den of thieves of Parlay Atoll was a mere three hours away from the New Providence harbor, or rather, the garrisoned fort. It must have made Flynn nervous knowing many of his old mates from the Brotherhood, the ones he'd crossed, which refused to accept the King's Pardon, lurked so close to his roost in the governor's mansion. 'Twas a burden enough having an uneasy accord with those buccaneers living in Nassau whom did accept the pardon. Though free men, they were none too pleased with Flynn capturing and hanging brethren under the protection of the Royal Navy. If it weren't for the fact that many colonists on New Providence were sympathetic to the pirates, he'd have sent Christensen to eradicate the island. But Flynn feared the act would trigger an uprising, as he should, and he enjoyed his affluent station too much to let that happen.

Many of Blackthorn's own men had come into the tavern to carouse. There wasn't much else to do on this spit of an island. A handful of establishments, a nanny-house, a very small, very empty church, and a woodsy jungle was all there was to be found.

Blackthorn had taken up a table in the corner with his back to the wall. Having this many dangerous scoundrels in one spot made for a pot ready to boil over. 'Twas tense and volatile. Best he be on high guard with a clear view of the room and the door. But only one individual in the tavern warranted his attention. Rathbone. Blackthorn had him rowed to shore as soon as they dropped anchor, then he removed his shackles and sent him on his way like a scurrying rat. Now the bastard sat one table over, glaring at him with evil designs. Let the wretch try and cross him. 'Twould be the last thing he did right before Blackthorn put a ball between his eyes.

A dusty beam of sunlight cut through the thick air as the front door opened. The shadow of a tall navy officer filled the threshold and the room fell silent. Blackthorn kept his hand on his piece, waiting.

"Stow your arm, Jackson," the officer said to the keep behind the counter. "I'm not here to make trouble." Back straight, strides deliberate, he made his way to Blackthorn's table. "How's the wind, my friend?"

"I joy to see you again, Christensen." Only when the commodore sat did Blackthorn remove his hand from his gun. "I see you received my message."

"You are bloody insane sailing the *Sanctum* that close to New Providence." He removed his hat. His blond hair cut shorter than Blackthorn remembered.

"My point was made, and here you are. How is Annabelle?"

"Desperate to bear me another child," he said.

"Ho, ho." Blackthorn slapped the tabletop. "Congratulations, mate. How many does that make? Four?"

Christensen chuckled and motioned to a serving girl. "She sends her love."

"She's a mighty fine woman, Robert. I wish you'd let me give her that fancy gown I'd gotten for her."

"You know she refused the dress." Christensen ordered two mugs of stout. "She wants you to come for Christmas instead. The boys liked the marbles you gave them."

Christensen was a lucky cockerel. He had a beautiful wife and three little bucks that adored him, with another on the way. Maybe he'll get a daughter this time. Blackthorn was happy for his friend. But deep inside, he was also envious. He could have been a commanding officer of the Royal Navy with a loving family, too. But he wasn't. Blackthorn was destined for a darker journey.

"They, too, want to see Uncle Bran."

"Well now, that depends on the charity of your governor, doesn't it?" Blackthorn knew it was highly unlikely he'd ever see the boys again. It pained him, but in time, they'd forget the "uncle" who had wrestled with them, took them rabbit hunting, and played endless hours of games with them.

Christensen huffed and leaned back in his chair. "Flynn's a damned difficult son of a bitch. He wants you dead."

"I could say the same about him."

"He can't kill you without having the whole confederacy of pirates setting about to destroy Nassau." The serving girl set their mugs between them. Christensen waited until she left, coins in hand, before continuing. "He doesn't want to give you a pardon, either. Flynn knows he's bent over a gun. He's waiting for you to give him a reason to send me after you." He paused. "I'm sorry, my friend. I never want to be put in that situation. I should have been rendezvousing with you months ago with a reprieve in hand."

"'Tis my burden, not yours." Blackthorn wouldn't dwell on what could have been, lest he become bitter. And he wasn't easy to get along with on his best days. "Besides, I've a little something to persuade Flynn."

"Oh? This should be interesting."

"I have in my possession a girl. A certain Mrs. Elyssa Calhoun Montgomery."

"Come now, Bran. Slavery? That's not like you. You've made slaves into free men."

"I may be above slavery, but not ransom." He waited for Christensen to catch up and took a long pull from his mug. The stout was good, robust. Blackthorn would likely order another round, especially for how long it took Christensen to put the pieces together.

"Blast it, Bran! This woman, she's of the Samuel Montgomery brood?"

Blackthorn shrugged. "Daughter-in-law."

"How did you—"

"It's not how it seems." He shot a look over to Rathbone. The scug was hunched over his ale, his jaw set tight, cutty-eyeing Blackthorn. Blackthorn should take the bastard outside and plug his fist into his cribbage-faced mug. "The details are unimportant."

"So you're hitting Flynn in his coffers. You'll send word to Montgomery's lawyer in Nassau announcing you have the woman and you'll release her unharmed, but only if the governor will issue the pardon."

Blackthorn avoided thinking too much on Elyssa's release. He never thought of himself as a man who could get high in the ropes over a woman. Yet he grappled with long forgotten emotions and visions of a smiling angel. The beast he'd cultivated over the years chanted unthinkable tactics in his mind, twining around his pirating creed—take all that he may. He was strong enough to bury those wicked ideas. But just barely.

"A pretty solid plan, wouldn't you say?"

"If Flynn refuses?"

"I will expect a king's price for her safe return." And return her, he would. He had to, for her own safety.

"'Tis a precarious perch you sit upon."

"As do you for coming here."

"What's life," Christensen grinned, "without a little excitement among brothers?"

"I'll drink a hearty one to that." He clanked his cup with Christensen.

Cross words interrupted their toast. Mac approached Rathbone and slammed his hands down onto Rathbone's table, spouting curses. Accusations and threats over Elyssa lobbed between the men. Tension wound tight as a windlass.

"So that's how you happened upon the girl," Christensen said, overhearing the squabble. "Dressed as a lad, was she? And here I thought you'd turned into a heartless kidnapper." He was clearly amused by Blackthorn's acquisition.

"Damn all. My reputation is compromised." They shared a chuckle and another drink.

"Annabelle wants to find you a wife, have you settle down. She hates the thought of you—" *Don't say lonely.* "—spending time in a brothel. She has a friend she wants you to make acquaintances with." Christensen wore a crooked grin. "I met the young woman. She's quite handsome, and a good huntswoman, too." He winked. "I know how much you like spirited maidens."

"Ha! You tell Annabelle I'm all right and I'm in no need of a companion of any sort."

"Oh? Did a woman capture the impervious Captain Blackthorn's heart?"

Stormed was a better assessment.

"Are...are you smiling?"

Was he?

"Ho, ho! A woman did get to you. Who is she? I've got to meet the lass who can make you enamored."

Blackthorn no longer smiled. "I'm not enamored. Besides, my lot is cast. She is unattainable and a hazard."

"That's not stopped you before." Christensen's mouth fell open and he blew out a sigh of realization. "She's the Montgomery girl, isn't she?"

"It matters not."

"Doesn't it?"

There was that look. That look Christensen failed miserably to hide. Pity for what had become of Blackthorn. Blackthorn wasn't destined to have a life like Christensen. He had accepted it, but his friend had not.

"I'll speak no more of it," Blackthorn said.

Rathbone shot up from his seat, knocking back his chair. The argument between the scab and Mac mounted.

"That one," Blackthorn nodded to Rathbone, "keep an eye lifting on him. He's a murderous wretch preying on women."

"You don't say." Christensen stared hard at the bastard. "Be a shame should he find trouble among my soldiers."

"Aye, a shame."

Rathbone took a menacing step forward, nose to nose with Mac.

"I best put an end to that," Blackthorn said, rising from the table. "Don't need my lad stirring up trouble for Jackson. Drop your anchor, mate, we'll finish our drinks and talk of finer things."

Blackthorn grabbed the men each by a shoulder and shoved them apart. "You boys need to ease off and mind your noise. They'll be no fighting here. Mac, go sit with the others and get yourself foxed."

Mac slid his gaze from Blackthorn to Rathbone, hate twisting his lips.

"Tumble to it, son," Blackthorn commanded.

Mac jostled past Rathbone and joined a group of *Sanctum* lads.

"You." Blackthorn swiveled to stand directly into front of Rathbone. "I advise you to sheer off lest I pipe-clay into you."

Rathbone struggled to keep his fury in check. That was evident in the vein throbbing upon his temple. He cast a glance to Christensen who leaned back and rested his hand on his saber.

"A word of counsel," Blackthorn added. "Don't let me see your arse again. I'm likely to make good on that judgment I promised you."

"Arsehole." Rathbone ground out his declaration through his rotting teeth.

Blackthorn guffawed. "You're too kind." His smile gone, he gave Rathbone one last order. "Now, see your way out."

The wharf rat turned on his heel and stalked out the tavern, slamming the door behind him. Somehow, slinking in the back of his mind, Blackthorn knew that wouldn't be the last time he saw Rathbone.

"Should I be worried, Kipp?"

Elyssa couldn't sit still in the longboat. She persistently turned around to get a better look at the island of scallywags.

"Nay, lass." Kipp rocked forward and back, slightly flicking his wrists, with each dip of the oars. "'Tis not safe here for a lass, but the capt'n won't let harm come to ya."

She wasn't sure what to think about that.

Sparkling azure water gave way to clear crystalline surf gently caressing brilliant white sands and dark flat rocks. Beyond the beach, large leafy green shrubs and trees swayed with the ocean breezes passing through. Yellow flowers dotted the landscape. A long line of brown pelicans soared silently overhead. The coastline was beautiful, to be sure. But beauty can be dangerous.

She upturned her face to the warmth of the sun. It felt good to be out of the confines of the captain's quarters.

"I want to thank you again, Kipp. I was not obliged to have my request for fresh air granted." She had merely wanted to be allowed on deck to stretch her legs and let the sun's rays dry her clammy skin. Kipp was ever so kind to ask for the permission to accompany her and, by some miracle, Bran had agreed. But instead of taking a walk around the *Sanctum*, she'd be taking a stroll along the beach with the captain.

Perhaps it wasn't the cutthroats nesting on the island that made her insides braid into knots. Perhaps it was finding herself alone with Bran again.

"He was gonna let ya outta there sooner or later." He leaned in as if imparting a secret. "Ya gone and charmed the capt'n, ya did." Kipp winked, and Elyssa couldn't stop her tittering grin.

"You think so?"

"Ask him yerself." He tipped his chin to the pier.

Bran stood at the end of the dock looking every bit as dash and daring as the day he seized the *Maraville*—dressed in his long black dress coat, long hair tied back, and strapped with a bandolier of pistols. 'Twas good she was sitting, for he made her weak-kneed.

"Ah, Mister Kipp. My gratitude for bringing Mrs. Montgomery ashore."

Elyssa climbed the ladder up and took Bran's outstretched hand to help her on the pier.

"Pleasure's mine, Capt'n," Kipp said. "But I'll be glad to take my leisure now, if ya don't mind."

"Of course, mate. Go get lost in your rudder."

Elyssa thanked Kipp again, and taking Bran's elbow, left the first mate tying up the boat.

Bran led them to the end of the pier and turned away from the cluster of buildings. He took a foot path running along the outer edge of the beach. The path gently sloped upward, but Bran kept his pace slow.

"This trail leads to a lookout up in the outcropping," Bran said. "'Tis a grand view I want to show you."

"That would be wonderful." Elyssa was certain she would bust at the seams with the many things she wanted to say. 'Twas foolish, but she wanted to share with him all her giddy feelings about him. She stole a glance up at his handsome profile. He, too, seemed as if he had something on his mind. Was it her? Could she dare ask? She decided to wait a little longer.

They strolled past an old cemetery overgrown with weeds and the shell of a crumbling hurricane-ravaged home. Bran explained bits of history behind Parlay Atoll. The rogues squatting there, both past and present, were men to be feared, violent and blood-thirsty. But in listening to Bran, she realized not all were the devil's spawn. Many had adventuresome tales, interesting lives, and a strong sense of duty to one another. Fascinating.

The ease with which he talked lulled her. Elyssa could wrap herself up in the comfort of their casual conversation. Being with him, it felt so … right. Excitement tickled within her.

"Here we are," Bran said.

'Twas more of a small ledge wedged between two palm trees than a lookout, but the view stole her breath. The glittering sea gave way to various shades of stunning blue. The beach below, as white as fresh snow on a crisp winter morning, curved along with the coastline, broken only by patches of black rock. They weren't so high that the steady murmurs of breaking surf didn't reach her ears. Islands rose from the horizon, much closer than she anticipated.

"Beautiful."

"Yes, she is."

Elyssa met his stare. She had that fluttering feeling in her stomach again.

He blinked and dropped his elbow from her hold. "That island there," he pointed to a large mass in the northwest. "That is New Providence." He leaned against a tree, plucking a red hibiscus from a nearby bush. "That is where you will find Montgomery's office."

"You're releasing me?"

Twirling the flower's stem between his fingertips, he said, "Soon."

She should be overjoyed. The pirate master was setting her free. And yet, Elyssa didn't want to be set free. Nay, that wasn't true. She wanted freedom, freedom to choose where to lay her head at night, and with whom. "What would you say if I told you I wanted to stay with you?"

Blackthorn's brow furrowed. "I'd say you've been tippling in my rum stash."

"I speak true, Bran. You're all I think about." Oh Lord, did her tongue run amok? She clamped her teeth onto her lip before she began to sound like an infatuated child.

"You don't know what you want, Elyssa." He threw the flower to the ground. "You've been at sea too long and only recently lost your husband. You're frightened of what awaits you out there."

He rolled to his shoulder on the tree and faced the ocean. Why was he angry at her? She steadied a fluster of humiliation with a deep breath of admission.

"You may be right," she said. "I don't know what I'm to do once I'm in Nassau. I'll have to send word to Lord Montgomery of Dobie and it will be months before I know if I'll be given an allowance. So yes, I'm a wee bit frightened. With you, I'm not so scared."

"You've cracked your skull."

She put her hand on his arm, warm and solid. "I would like more time with you, Bran."

He tilted his chin, looking down upon her. Irritation, pity, lust, she couldn't decipher what was going on in his coppery eyes, but they were alive with emotion. He pushed off the tree. "You don't know what you are asking." He annunciated each word slowly.

She rose to her tiptoes, lessening the distance between their gazes, between the doorways of their souls, so that he might see her heart. "I know exactly what I'm asking." By saints, she did.

"Damn it, woman," he growled.

Bran snatched Elyssa and pulled her tight against his chest. She gasped, wetting her parted lips with her tongue. He was hungry for those lips, more hungry than he had ever been. He had no strength of will left. It had been scuttled and ruthlessly sunk to the depths of the ocean with her last declaration. "Damn it." With no more control, he crushed his mouth to hers.

She muddled his mind, and for that moment, Bran did not care about consequence. He'd be the pirate he was meant to be. He'd take what he could, what she would give, while there was still time left. And why not? The good Lord knew the sands of Bran's hourglass were running out. Hell was waiting.

Gently he guided Elyssa to the ground. He broke from their kiss and gazed upon her. The dying sunlight was captured in the amber strands of her tresses. A smile most innocent embellished her plump, flushed lips. She was more enchanting lying beneath him in the windswept grass than a chest full of precious gems and gleaming gold.

"I know exactly what I want, Bran. Don't make me beg. 'Twould be a dreadful sight." Elyssa cupped her hand behind his neck, pulling him down for a sensual kiss. Earthy scents of crushed foliage mingled with French soap. Sticky and sweet, their lips clung together for a brief stretch as she slowly released him.

By thunder, Blackthorn could take no more. He sat back on his heels and removed his coat and both bandoliers of pistols. "What a bewitching spell you have cast upon me. I have never come across anything like you, Elyssa. Not in all my wretched life."

"And you never will again," she smirked.

Somewhere between madness and rapture he succumbed and descended upon her. Tugging her bodice down, a seam popped. It took all his might to slow down, to not rip her clothes. The beast in him wanted to tear away every scrap of clothing she wore from her body. *Control, Bran. Maintain your control.*

With her breasts bare from restraints, he took her taut bosom into his mouth. He flicked his tongue across the hard peak. Her fingers threaded tight through his hair, her breathing quickened. Christ, her sighs pleased him in a way he did not understand. He wanted her to enjoy this as much as he.

Desperate, but not willing to leave her delectable breasts yet, he grabbed fistfuls of her dress, pulling, tugging the folds—too many damn folds—up around her waist. She must've felt the same desperation, for Elyssa helped, grabbing her own bunches of fabric. The smooth naked skin of her inner thigh was sleek as alabaster stone against his palm. He surrendered her breast for a taste of her leg.

Blackthorn nudged her legs open and planted himself between them. For one long moment, he gazed upon her exposed mound. What treasures she beheld there. He admired the view, migrating to her puckered nipples and still further to her white teeth gnawing that bottom lip. He was certain his lass had not experienced what he was about to do next. Worry lines drew at her brow.

He kissed her thigh very near the heat of her core.

"Bran."

He kissed the other thigh and dragged his tongue closer.

"Bran. Oh!"

She tasted of warmth, fleshy and fresh, a wine of the gods. He suckled and kissed her folds, swirling his tongue on her nub. Moans and references to all that was holy encouraged him further. Her hands alternated from grabbing his head to slamming down to snatch clumps of grass. Elyssa rotated her hips to the flick of his tongue until her thighs tensed and her knees clamped around his head. She screamed out. Music, the most divine music he had ever heard.

Urgent need pressed tight against his trousers. He needed release. Blazes! He needed to be inside her. He'd have her scream again, soon.

Blackthorn kissed the inside of her thigh again before prowling up her body. Hovering above her, he grinned. "How did you like that, my angel?"

Elyssa struggled to catch her breath. "Oh my…Bran… I've never… You…"

He gave her a reprieve and kissed her. The heady taste on his lips shared with her unraveled him. His cock grew harder, if that were possible. With one hand, and faster than the drop of an anchor, he freed himself from his breeches.

"I don't deserve the gift you bestow, here, with me," he said. The wet flesh of her core readily received him and he eased inside. "But I will cherish it always." She said his name on a wispy breath arching her back as he slid deeper within.

Her glassy eyes gazed at him, so full of lov—desire. "As will I," she said.

Taking both her hands, he laced his fingers with hers. In and out, he rocked. Slowly at first, then as a ship sails into tumultuous seas, he picked up speed, pitching and bucking along to Elyssa's throaty voluptuous cries. With each thrust, the pressure in his cock built. He bristled, smoldered, ready to explode from the sensitivity of pumping into her.

She squeezed his hands, flung her legs around his waist, and cried out. The friction she created coupled with her quivering muscles drove him blind. He bit out a growl on one final jab and erupted. He was rendered immobilized, unable to do anything more than collapse into the arms of the woman who had stowed away into his heart, until the waves of pleasures ceased.

Stowed away into his heart? 'Twas unwise to entertain ideas of ardent affairs. Regret would be his due. *Ah, but not for long.*

Elyssa craned her neck up to kiss him. "Thank you," she whispered against his lips.

He answered by taking her mouth, chaste and tender and then withdrawing.

Words were not spoken as they redressed. But Blackthorn found it comforting as none were needed. Together they sat on the bluff and looked out over the horizon. She moved close, and before he realized it, he had wrapped his arm around her waist. Aye, being with her was too comfortable.

"Watch the sky," he said. "The colors of sunsets in the Caribbean are the most beautiful you've ever seen." From the corner of his eye, he saw her glance at him and smile.

Shades of yellows and oranges along the horizon's edge gave way to dark hues of pinks. Purple tinged the dawdling clouds. Rays of light speared out from behinds the billows.

"Amazing," she said. She rested her head on his shoulder. "These last two hours, with you, have been amazing."

He agreed. 'Twould be hard to top this afternoon. But he bloody well would try. "Tonight, love, I will reclaim my bed. And you will be in it. Naked."

She spooled her arm around his. "Yes, Captain."

A strange feeling bloomed within his chest. 'Twas not easy to ignore, but he must try. She would be gone soon enough, and so would he.

"We'd better get back." He helped her to her feet. "It'll be dark soon and I'd hate to shoot anyone who might think to try their luck on robbing us."

"Too bad. It is breathtaking here."

"Not as breathtaking as you, my angel."

Nighttime birds, frogs and insects had begun their choruses and the breeze carried in cooler air as they descended down the hill. He escorted her with his hand resting on top of hers, caressing her knuckles to alleviate any fear she might have of the dark now shrouding them. Blackthorn's sense of duty to protect her from anyone or anything was fierce, more so than to his men or, at one time, his country. He would have it no other way.

They broke from the copse of jungle and strolled through the sands of the beach. Flaming torches marking the buildings to the pirate haven came into view. A cacophony of music and guffawing drunkards wafted over the waves rolling in. Instinctively, he kissed her temple. What had she done to him?

"I think it's time to retire, Captain Blackthorn."

A devilish grin rose to the impish sparkle in her eyes. Glory be, he had an insatiable lass. He now knew for certain Elyssa wasn't a curse. Nor was she a blessing. The bonny girl was both. "I verily believe you are right, my dear. It is time to retire."

She giggled. "Race you to the pier."

Before he could stop her, Elyssa ran toward the dock. "No!" Tufts of sand kicked up from her heels. She was mighty quick of foot and Blackthorn, heavier than she, labored to catch up in the deep sand. "Elyssa, stop!" The fool girl. Had she forgotten she was on a cutthroat island?

A man stumbled out from behind a stack of barrels, smacking into Elyssa.

"Shit!" Blackthorn drew a pistol and was upon them in an instant.

The man yanked her into his chest and raised his pistol to Blackthorn. "Stay back!" he hollered.

"Get off her handsomely or get a bullet in your skull."

Elyssa squirmed to get out of his grasp until she looked into the man's face. "Mac?"

Mac? Hell, Blackthorn didn't recognize the lad.

"Dear Lord, Mac," she said. "You're hurt."

Keeping his pistol aimed at the paddy, Blackthorn walked closer to get a better look at him. Mac's face had been mangled. His eyes were red and near swollen shut. Dried blood matted his russet hair and caked around his crooked nose. A crack split his bottom lip. Mac had taken a terrible beating.

Elyssa reached up to touch Mac's face, but he flinched away. "What happened to you?"

"That Rathbone, he ambushed me." He kept his stare on Blackthorn. Elyssa stepped free of him. "Put up a good fight, I did. Until the bastard came at me with an oar." His speech was thick, slurred from his fattened jaw. "Has he harmed you, Elysen?"

"What? No." Surprise surfaced as she realized her friend and Blackthorn still pointed their weapons at each other.

"Lay down your piece, son," Blackthorn commanded.

"It's all right, Mac. Captain Blackthorn isn't going to hurt me."

"That so." Mac snorted. "If it's all the same to you, I'll decline."

Blackthorn was certain the fellow sent daggers through his marred scowl. "Lay down your piece," he repeated.

"I'll not omit to tell you what that wretch Rathbone spouted about. The captain, here, got a ransom on yer head, Elysen. Sure and certain."

"I don't understand."

"He expects to be paid for ya."

Confusion hemmed into her brow. "What is he talking about, Bran?"

Blackthorn lowered his flintlock. Rathbone must have overheard his conversation with Christensen. Damn! And now, something she was never meant to know had been laid open. She was a pawn in a deadly game and she would never forgive him.

"Bran?"

"I'm sorry, Elyssa. You gave me no choice."

"Me?"

"The daughter-in-law of Lord Samuel Montgomery on my ship, a pirate ship, offers an opportunity to act upon." Why couldn't he bring himself to lie to her? It would save her from the sting of the truth. "You must understand how complicated—"

"You used me."

The tears welling in her eyes crushed him. Blackthorn couldn't bear to witness her disappointment and chose to look to his shoes instead. He never expected his burdens could become heavier with the weight of guilt, but it had. It was a different kind of guilt. Not from the death of a foolheaded boy. Something worse. Hurting the woman who had brought his heart to its knees.

"Oh, God." She hugged herself. "You and I...I thought you...thought I was..." Rivulets of tears flowed down her cheeks, her nose reddened. "You used me then, too."

"No."

"You bastard!"

Her words struck him hard. He'd been called worse, deserved worse. But coming from her lips, a cutlass through his gut would hurt less than the pain he felt now.

"You foresworn, envenomed bastard!"

Elyssa spun and fled toward the lighted buildings.

"Elyssa!"

He should have gone after her, he wanted to. But he didn't. He just watched as she ran away. Perhaps, for the first time in his life, he was a coward. He was afraid for Elyssa. His selfishness had put her in grave danger. He was scared of keeping her close, and scared of letting her go. But mostly, he was terrified of his true feelings for her. By thunder, what had become of him?

Mac shook his head, pity and anger framed his downturned blistered mouth.

"Best go after her, son," Blackthorn said. "She can't be alone here."

Mac turned to leave. He grabbed the fellow's shoulder, stopping him. Blackthorn fished a coin from his waistcoat. "For board."

The Irish lad looked to his hand. Incredulously, he nodded.

"And, Mac. Please keep her safe."

CHAPTER 8

"You sure this is gonna work, Blackthorn? Comin' here, without the girl?"

Kipp leaned against the white column of Nassau's government building keeping a keen watch for soldiers and other enemies. He spun his knife over and around his knuckles, completely at ease and hardly putting any effort at all into it. Blackthorn, resting his hand on the cutlass at his hip, nodded to folks who chanced a look at him and his mate, quickening their steps as they crossed before them. Ah, their fear usually put him in good humor. Not today.

"Nay, Kipp," Blackthorn admitted. "I'm not sure."

In the square, people bustled in and out of colorful shops and around the many vendor stands. Hawkers peddling their wares called out to passersby. Hooves from horses pulling carriages clopped on the cobblestones. Fresh bread wafted through the air from the nearby bakery. From his vantage on the steps, Blackthorn had a clear view down the avenue to the docks—a good distance away should escape become necessary. Not that he planned an escape. Just so long as his men could make it to open waters if something were to go wrong. One shot in the air would alert his man down by the docks to send the signal for the *Sanctum* to set sail—without Blackthorn.

"Even if the lass crossed over from Parlay Atoll and found Montgomery's officer, Flynn will not know I no longer have her. Not yet," Blackthorn said.

"Awful risky, mate."

"Just how you like it, eh?"

Kipp chuckled. "And it ain't even Christmas."

It took great effort to smile at his friend's joke. Nothing would crack Blackthorn's sour mood. After he had lost Elyssa last night, he could think of nothing but her. She invaded his every thought, lacerating him with visions of crestfallen tears. He had paced his chambers until he could take no more and drowned himself in liquor till he strayed from consciousness. Dear Neptune, he paid for it now. A dull throb grated incessantly in his head and his mouth tasted of nappy wool. He couldn't let that stop him from his mission.

"You should get down to the docks if you're going to make it back to the ship."

"I told ya, I ain't goin'." Kipp tipped his hat to a handsome woman strolling past. "Somebody's got to cover yer arse."

"It wasn't a request, mate. It's an order."

"Guess this here is what ya call a mutiny, b'cause I ain't goin'."

"Stubborn fool."

A valet, stiff from proper convention and dressed completely in white, exited the front door of the government house. "Governor Flynn will see you now," he said.

Blackthorn leaned into to the man, a devilish grin crooking up his mouth. "Tell me, snip, how do you feel about showing a blood-thirsty pirate about? Make you nervous, does it?"

The valet shrank a step back "Uh. Ahem. C-C-Commodore Christensen is here, sir."

Good. Just what Blackthorn wanted to hear, though he might have just asked the lad. Poor fellow looked as if he messed his trousers. With Christensen there, Blackthorn knew Flynn did indeed choose to meet with him instead of arresting him outright. "Well, show the way, then."

The valet gathered the shards of his composure and led them around the porch.

Flynn sat at a table overlooking a rose garden, sipping tea. Overdressed for the heat in a heavily embroidered cream coat, mountainous white-wig, and flaunting his wealth on burnished fingers, Flynn was a disgraceful sight bloated on self-importance. Blackthorn acknowledged Christensen, who stood close by, with a nod.

"Captain Blackthorn." Flynn addressed Blackthorn without the courtesy of looking at him. Nor did he offer him a seat.

"A fair morning, Your Honor," Blackthorn said, perhaps a little heavy with sarcasm on *Your Honor*.

"Tell me Captain, what do you think of my roses? Stunning, aren't they?"

"If you don't mind the thorns, I suppose," Blackthorn said.

"I sit out here everyday to enjoy them. The reds, yellows, whites, quite elegant, wouldn't you say?" The governor didn't wait for Blackthorn to answer. "They must be cared for meticulously. Spent flowers should be pinched off, branches trimmed, water maintained. Do these and the garden will flourish. But the flowers are susceptible to pests and left untreated would destroy the plants. Pests must be eliminated for the sake the garden. Do you understand?"

"Sounds as if you are threatening me."

Flynn finally looked up to Blackthorn. "Take it as you like, pirate."

The governor said pirate as if the very word tasted bitter and repugnant on his lips. *Hypocrite*.

"My occupation is just a worthy as yours, *Governor*, and, given how you acquired your position, more honorable."

"Gentlemen." Christensen stepped forward. "Threats and slander will cause a stalemate. Let us remember why we are here."

"Ah, yes. The matter of a pardon." Flynn took a sip from his delicate porcelain teacup. His cool apathetic manner set Blackthorn's teeth to grind. He wanted to shove that teacup down his pompous gullet.

"For the *Sanctum*."

"And to ensure I give you—"

"The *Sanctum*," Blackthorn corrected.

"—the *Sanctum* a pardon, you will hold this," he twirled his hand in the air, "girl ransom."

"We both know Samuel Montgomery is a Lord Proprietor of the Bahamas. He has the power to pull the purse strings shut on New Providence. And remove you from your lofty throne as a powerless governor. Do you want to risk denying my request for a reprieve?"

He shrugged. "There are other financiers."

"Who would trust their money to a man who cannot make diplomatic decisions? Who offers pardons discriminately and in doing so risks the whole of the Coast Brotherhood bearing down on you? Don't tell me you've forgotten how unforgiving the brethren can be when one of their own has been wronged. Don't tell me you've forgotten what happened in Petit-Goâve, the hangings, the roastings. Nassau will burn. What will become of your precious roses then, Flynn?"

Kipp chuckled. At least his quartermaster found the humor in the irony. Flynn didn't seem to appreciate it as much.

"Now it is you threatening me."

"Take it as you like, *brother*."

If the wastrel could summon the elements, Blackthorn had no doubt Flynn would have a black, swirling tempest bearing down upon them. Lucid hate roiled off him in crashing waves.

"I could have you executed."

"And I could kill you where you sit."

"'Twould solve nothing," Christensen interjected. He looked directly at Blackthorn. Severity leveled his brow but his eyes pleaded for Blackthorn to proceed carefully.

So be it. "Make a decision, Flynn."

A potted palm at the corner of the porch crashed to the white painted floor.

"You, sir! Stop!" Flynn's valet screeched. "You can't go back there!"

Blackthorn, Kipp, and Christensen drew their pistols aiming for whoever came around the corner. Flynn grabbed the arms of his chair, wide-eyed and frightened and ready to make a run for it. Porcelain clinked as his knees hit the table. Criminy. Being governor had made him softer than Blackthorn originally thought. Of course, with all the enemies Flynn had accumulated throughout the years, he *should* be frightened.

Mac stumbled up short, his hands raised to show he was unarmed.

"My apologies, Your Honor," the valet said. "He wouldn't listen to reason."

"Capt'n Blackthorn," Mac said between gasps for breath.

"Damn near got a plug in your brisket, son," Blackthorn said.

"He's one of yours?" Christensen asked.

"I picked him up recently." He holstered his gun. "But he's done no wrong." Blackthorn wanted it known the Irish lad was free of any crimes, if only because Elyssa trusted him. He would be a free man unbound by a pirate creed, regardless of what happened to the *Sanctum* crew.

Christensen gave Blackthorn a subtle nod. The man was astute and understood him perfectly.

Flynn relaxed back into his chair. "Get this rubbish out of here."

Mac shook his head excitedly and sidestepped around Christensen. "He got her, Capt'n."

Blackthorn didn't have a good feeling. What was Mac doing here? Why had he sought him out? Was he talking about Elyssa?

"You've got to help her." Sweat beaded on the wrinkles of desperation pleating his brow.

Kipp scowled. "Speak plain, lad."

"Rathbone."

Blackthorn's chest grew tight. His vision constricted, as if he wore blinders. Everything around him, the roses, the tea set, the other men, faded into a blur. *Elyssa!*

"Rathbone," Mac repeated. "He took Elysen."

Kipp spouted profanity.

In two strides, Blackthorn grabbed Mac. "Where?"

"Is this the Montgomery girl?" Christensen asked.

"Aye, Commodore," Kipp replied.

Blackthorn glanced to Christensen. Concern hemmed across his forehead.

"Where?" Blackthorn shook Mac. "Where did he take her? When? Answer me."

"I…I…"

Thoughts of rape and murder ran rampant in his mind, darting out between dark recesses and muddling his reasoning. Rathbone's filthy hands on his woman, *his woman*, were too much to brook. He had to get to her. Now! "Answer me!"

"Ease off, Blackthorn."

Blackthorn shrugged off Christensen's hand on his shoulder.

"It's all right, lad," Christensen said, undaunted by Blackthorn's trenchant gesture. "Tell us what you know. What happened to Mrs. Montgomery?"

Wild-eyed, Mac swallowed, looking between them all, before he settled back on Blackthorn. Blackthorn let him go and Mac shuffled a step back. "We were in the square, on our way to the Montgomery office. She saw you and Mister Kipp up here on the porch like you were waitin' for someone. She wanted to speak to you. But as we got near, Rathbone popped out of the alley, stole her away, he did. I'd tried to give chase, but lost 'em in the crowd."

If ever Blackthorn practiced control, this was the time. "Which way did they head?" he managed to ground out.

"The docks."

Blackthorn shoved Mac to the side.

"You've got to help her, Capt'n!"

Blackthorn was already gone by the time Mac finished his last word. Kipp, Christensen, they called after him, but he didn't stop. By thunder, would he stop. Flynn and his pardon could go to hell. It no longer mattered. Only Elyssa mattered. He ran, not bothering with porch steps, jostling past people strolling along the streets, knocking over the cart a fruit vendor had pushed in his path.

He paused at the docks, his heart drumming against his ribs. To his right were the wharves, dockyard, and warehouses. Men milled about loading and unloading ships. Sawing and hammering from the shipyard added to the noise of creaking windlasses and shouted orders from overseers. To his left, just beyond the chandler, beyond the fishing crates and nets, a sliver of beach disappeared into a craggy rim of a lagoon. There! Rathbone had to have taken her there. No one would hear a woman scream on the other side of the rocky wall.

Blackthorn jumped over a stack of crates and followed the wooden dock until it ended. His boots sunk into the soft sand slowing his progress. Only once he reached the rocky barrier did he stop. His lungs burned from the exertion and he needed to catch his breath, to harness his sensibility. He could not be undisciplined. Elyssa's life depended on it. He had to hunt down Rathbone, assess the situation, and save his bonny lass. There was no other option.

Voices carried over the embankment, Blackthorn had to move.

To get around the wall, Blackthorn would have to wade out into the surf. That was not favorable, as he would likely be seen. He'd have to find a way around through the dense tropical jungle. Vines and mangroves were thick. Aggravation at having to tramp through the leafy tangle unfurled his prudence. *Burn this!* He began to climb the rugged wall. The jagged stones cut into his fingers and stabbed his palms and his waistcoat hindered his hand over hand ascent. His boots scraped against the rock, slipping until a toehold could be found. By God, he would get to the top.

The breeze on the ridge cooled the sweat trickling down his temple. He dusted off the pebbles stuck into his palms onto his trousers and looked for any sign of Elyssa or that bilge rat, Rathbone. Sunlight skimmed across the gentle waves lapping the shore. Black boulders lined the crusty sand. Blackthorn searched along the rim of the inlet. Below, almost out of his line of sight, he caught a glimpse of movement. He scaled down the embankment, careful not to dislodge loose rocks. Closer, a stone's cast away, Elyssa and Rathbone came into view.

Elyssa's wrists were bound and bloodied by a length of rope and the wretch was having a devil of a time tying her to a tree. He tried to secure her hugging the tree, undoubtedly to defile her with ease, but she fought, twisted and writhed with all her might. Rathbone pressed his body into hers to minimize her struggles. Blackthorn clenched his fists. *Keep calm. Keep fucking calm.*

"I'll gut ya now if ya don't stop." Rathbone's knife glinted in the sunlight as he pulled it from his waist and flashed it before her eyes.

Blackthorn got a clear look of Elyssa's tear-stained face. Rage boiled up, heat singed his neck. He held his breath, his jaw aching from grinding his teeth. An unsightly bruise had formed under her eye. He was going to kill that maggot, spit on his worthless carcass for harming her.

Rathbone threw the rope over a branch and yanked her arms over her head. Pain shot from her raw wrists down to her shoulder blades. She stomped on his foot.

"Ow!" Rathbone slapped her. "Keep fightin' me, chit. I'm gonna watch ya bleed."

He flattened his slovenly body in closer, his scarred, blotched face an inch from hers. The edge of his dagger pricked the skin under her chin and all but guaranteed she wouldn't move again.

"I finally get to bury m'self in ya." His putrid breath stung her nose. She swallowed back the bile burning at the back of her throat. "Make ya scream. Make ya beg me not to hurt ya no more. But I'm not gonna show mercy on ya. No. I like my doxies to suffer." He dragged his slimy tongue up her cheek. She squeezed her eyes shut.

Elyssa could think of no way to escape this madman. No way but death. He planned to kill her anyway. Could she talk her way through this? Perhaps tell him lies, become a willing participant, gain his trust until he untied her and flee at the first chance? Was he that stupid? Nay, she would rather welcome a quick death than submit to the atrocities Rathbone intended. If only he would turn his dagger a little more, she could impale her own throat.

She would not make this easy for him. The sooner she angered him, the sooner she'd find peace.

Rathbone smashed his lips to her mouth. It took every particle of her being not to vomit. She bit his lip instead—hard—and wouldn't let go. He jerked away, but not before she tasted the metallic tang of his blood.

"Bitch!"

He struck her with the back of her hand.

Her head whipped to the side, tears snipped from her eyes at the smarting on her cheek. *Anger him more.* Elyssa slowly leveled an icy stare at him and spat in his face. "Flog off."

She braced herself as he raised his hand to strike her again.

"Does striking a woman make you feel like more of a man, Rathbone?"

Bran?

Rathbone spun around. "You." Spite dripped from his tone.

Elyssa's heart did a flip. He'd come for her. Her wicked pirate had come for her. *Hold on, Elyssa. He came for you to collect a ransom. Not because he has the same feelings for you as you do for him.*

Bran hopped down from a boulder and strode near with menacing ease. Even in the bright morning rays, the captain commanded the shadows. The rocks, the deep green foliage, even the water seemed to darken around him.

"See, I think you're a lily-livered coward," Bran said. "You prey on women and ambush men too drunk to put up a real fight."

"I ain't never seen ya in a brawl." Rathbone cocked his head with a contentious sneer. "Some capt'n, always lettin' that lackey of yers, Kipp, do all the scufflin'."

"A good leader is a tactical one," Bran retorted. "Shame you don't know more about me. 'Tis a regret you'll learn soon enough."

"Save yer cowing. Ya don't scare me."

Rathbone was a fool not to be intimidated by Bran. If Elyssa were the wretch, her knees would be knocking with fear.

"I've no intention to scare you, just kill you."

The blade of Bran's cutlass scraped against metal as Bran withdrew his sword from its scabbard. In a blur of speed, he swung the sword. Rathbone ducked away and the blade sliced through Elyssa's binds. She collapsed to the ground. Her arm muscles cricked from the release of being extended, but her wrists still chafed in their fetters.

A subtle grin broke across Bran's calm visage. "But first, are you man enough to fight me?"

"I've no sword. You've an advantage. Wouldn't be *honorable* of ya, now would it, Capt'n?"

Bran chuckled. "Honor has nothing to do with it. But I do like my opponent to be a mite challenging." His smile faded. "No weapons, Rathbone. We fight fist to fist. Or are you a coward?"

Rathbone clucked. "I've wanted to plug ya in the face since joinin' yer worthless crew."

The men threw their weapons aside and shed out of their jackets and tunics. Rathbone was a stocky man with a good build. No doubt he could dominate in a fracas. But Bran, his expansive muscular arms were impressive. Not because of how firm they felt under her fingertips. Not because her heart had been laid open to him. But because brawn such as his harnessed mighty power. Trails of embossed veins traced down his arms as he clenched and unclenched his fists.

Elyssa scrambled to her feet, putting the tree between her and them. Rathbone circled Bran, as if he were stalking prey. Bran moved only his eyes, watching his foe. Chills swept across Elyssa's flesh. Dear Lord, these men were going to pummel one another.

Rathbone swung first, but Bran deflected with his arm and delivered a blow under the cur's chin. Elyssa cringed at the sound of teeth crunching. Rathbone spat out a tooth and swung again, this time hitting his mark. Bran worked his jaw back and forth. Was...was he...smiling? He returned with another cracking blow. More strikes were traded. Solid jabs coming one after the other. How did they continue to throw punches unaffected by the bashing each took? Grunts tallied growls. Sand kicked up from their macabre dance. Won't they ever tire?

Rathbone veered away from Bran's swing and grappled him. They struggled, arms intertwined, wrestling, as Rathbone tried to bring Bran down. Bran plowed his knuckles into the exposed part of Rathbone's neck, crumpling him to the ground. Rathbone scampered away on all fours, sand flurrying up from his heels. Clambering to his feet, he snatched up a piece of driftwood and whacked Bran. Bran blocked but stumbled back, giving Rathbone just enough time to retrieve his gulley knife.

"Bran! Watch out!" *Oh God! No!*

Bran looked up too late. Rathbone charged him, locking into Bran in another powerful struggle. They grunted, arms trembling, from the exertion. Neither gained purchase. Elyssa's heart stopped. Blood wept from a gash in Bran's gut. The knife in Rathbone's clutch dripped red.

Mother of heaven! He's been stabbed. She must do something to help Bran. Anything! But what could she do with her wrists still bound? Bran's sword lay in the sand out of reach. Alack! She wouldn't be able to get around the fighting men to retrieve it. She looked all around her, nothing but rocks. Rocks everywhere. *Think, Elyssa, think!* She picked up a stone, round like a cannonball, but not quite as heavy. Running up behind them, she smacked the rock over Rathbone's head as hard as she could. 'Twasn't hard enough. The thud to his head stunned Rathbone, and he slipped away from Bran. Bran staggered backwards, his face drawn and blanched, looking down at his wound.

Rathbone sulked around. Malice kindled in his sneer. He kneaded the handle of his knife. "Ya shouldn't have done that, puss."

"You didn't fight fair."

"Ain't no rules in killin'."

Bran's eyes closed. His tense body swayed. He couldn't be dying, could he? Elyssa prayed it wasn't so.

Rathbone crept closer. "Now it's yer turn." He raised his blade. Elyssa chunked the rock at him as he lunged.

A shot rang out, echoing off the walls on the inlet. Rathbone froze, dagger in midair, eyes wide. He folded to his knees.

Smoke from the pistol Bran held dissipated in the breeze. "I told you I'd kill you." He strode over to the fiend and snatched the blade from his grip. Rathbone slumped to the ground.

Elyssa raced to Bran. He pulled her into an embrace and she held him tight, not minding the blood and sweat of his skin sticking to her.

"Elyssa." Her name on his lips, raspy yet tender, sounded of pure music. For one moment she allowed herself to soak into him, to move with him as he breathed heavily, thankful she was alive—thankful *he* was alive.

He'd done a treacherous thing to her, toying with her affections, using her for money and for her body. The hurt, she'd never experienced anything like it. She had cried until she had no more tears, felt her heart wither and die. If it hadn't been for Mac keeping close, she'd have walked into the sea and let the pull of the tides wash her away. She had wanted to hate Bran. Desperately. But she couldn't. Instead, she forgave him. Even if she was his pawn.

Her captivity at the mercy of a pirate could have been far worse. Quite frankly, she doubted lying beneath another man could ever make her feel the way he did. She had to believe she was fortunate. By all accounts, she should be dead thrice over. Now she could face her life unafraid to take risks. She would see Lord Montgomery's officer and build her shipping business, for she had nothing else to lose. In the meantime, she must guard her heart from Bran.

She pried out of his cradle. "We need to get you to a doctor." Blood coursed down the cut of his flank, staining the waist of his trousers.

Bran paid her no mind. He sliced through the rope at her wrists with Rathbone's dagger. "Are you all right? Did he hurt you?" He gingerly inspected her wrists.

"I'm fine. Please, Bran. You're bleeding badly."

"Capt'n!" Kipp climbed down the ragged wall jutting out into the surf. Mac followed on his heels.

A Royal Navy officer and another man stood atop the peninsula. This other man was impeccably dressed in flashy cream and yellow finery, dripping in jewelry, and wearing a full-bodied white wig with three masses of curls. Despite the wig had fallen out of fashion years ago, there was something else about him that held Elyssa's attention. He seemed familiar in some way. The distance between them kept her from distinguishing why.

Kipp and Mac jumped into the surf and waded the rest of the way to the beach.

"Elysen!" Mac said. "You all right, lass?"

"Yes." She met Mac as he came from the water, grabbed his hands, and gave a tight squeeze. "Thanks to you."

"Kipp," she joined the first mate. "Bran is hurt."

Kipp cast nothing more than a glance to Rathbone as he passed by his lifeless body.

"Just need a shot of rum, is all," Bran said.

Kipp crinkled his brow, giving Bran's wound a once over. "Like hell, mate. That's a nasty notch ya got there. We need to get it dressed 'fore ya bleed yourself dry."

"He could die?" *God, no. Won't this nightmare end?*

"Doncha worry none, lass. Death don't want Blackthorn. He's too much trouble."

Bran chuckled, though his smile was forced. It was too much for him. She was not fooled. He was in a lot of pain.

Bran cupped her chin, his eyes diving deep into her soul. "I'll be fine. I promise." He lied. She saw it in the twinge of his lids.

He kissed her on her forehead and turned to Kipp. "Let's go finish this," he said, jerking his head toward the men descending back down the other side of the ridge.

"Finish what? You need a doctor," she insisted.

Bran swooped her up and carried her out into the water.

"Please, Bran. You'll hurt yourself further." His face drew tight with the strain of carrying her. Elyssa tried not to move, tried to will herself to be lighter. "Kipp. Tell him to put me down."

Kipp just shook his head, swiped up his captain's belongings, and followed after them.

Bran set her feet onto the rocks. Thankful to no longer be a burden, she climbed over to the other side.

The officer, the gentleman, and several soldiers were waiting.

Soldiers? Needles of suspicion pricked at the recess of her mind. Something wasn't right. Were they there to arrest a pirate captain? Bran was close behind her, climbing down, telling her to watch her step. He was quite unconcerned by the soldiers. Perhaps, they were there to pay her ransom?

She should run.

And she might have if she could have stopped staring at the foppishly dressed man. Why was he so familiar? It hit her then. She twirled around to Bran joining her. Could it be? Bran and this man had the same dark eyes, same nose, same strong jaw. Why, they even shared the same smug smile. With the exception the man was slighter of build and perhaps a little older, and that ridiculously exaggerated wig, he looked nearly identical to Bran. So much so, they had to be brothers.

Bran addressed the men. "Governor Flynn. Commodore Christensen. May I present Mrs. Elyssa Calhoun Montgomery?"

Governor? This doesn't make sense. Bran is ransoming me to a governor?

The governor grazed her with a contemptible scowl and curled his lips as if she were nothing more than street rubbish.

Commodore Christensen offered her a bow of his head. "A pleasure, Mrs. Montgomery." He smiled and slid a glimpse to Bran.

What the devil was going on?

CHAPTER 9

"Seize the girl," Governor Flynn ordered.

Me? Did she hear him correctly?

"You'll do no such thing." Bran blocked anyone from coming near. "She stays with me." Kipp and Mac crowded in behind them.

"I'll go with no one." Her statement fell on deaf ears

"You're in no position to bargain with me, Blackthorn. Your cavalier design failed."

Kipp handed Bran his tunic. "Nay, Flynn," he said, shrugging back into his shirt. "You know well enough that when adversity lies off your ship's bow, you change course. I've always got another plan."

"I'll not be a part of your parlor games." Still no one paid Elyssa heed. Infuriating!

"Like after you shamed Father and were removed from the Royal Navy?" Governor Flynn challenged Blackthorn with a raised eyebrow.

So they *were* brothers.

Bran tilted his head passively. "More like when I overtook the Spanish galleon you'd laid claim to. I should never have told you about her. But then you always were trying to out best me."

The governor once was a pirate, too? Egads, things had gotten thorny. What spider's web had she become entangled in?

Governor Flynn's glare could pierce armor. "Best a gallows bird? Not likely."

"Oh, I disagree. It ate you up inside knowing our father had any amount of pride for me."

"Until you turned rogue."

"How long did you chase her?" Bran continued, ignoring Flynn's jab. "Eight days? Ho, ho! Your persistence and my patience paid off. I'm still toasting to you, from my golden chalice pilfered from the ship, of course, for such an easy quarry."

"Kill him." Venom spurt from the governor's angry demand. Red splotchy patches appeared on his face.

Kipp and Mac went for their pistols prompting the soldiers to do the same.

Commodore Christensen raised his hand to stay his men. "I can't do that without a reason, sir," he said to Governor Flynn.

"He's a pirate."

"With respect, Your Honor, I've no proof of that. It is hearsay."

"Right, that," Kipp piped up. "Just as 'tis hearsay you were once a pirate, eh, Gov'ner?"

Kipp could have benefited from a shield. Surely Flynn meant to destroy him with his raging eyes alone. "I was a privateer, cretin."

A sour smirk spread across Bran's lips. "Privateer, pirate, one and the same in the eyes of many. And depending on his mood, including the crown."

The governor snarled at the commodore. "Arrest him for murder. You *can* do that, can't you, Commodore? Is a dead body proof enough for you?"

"You can't!" Elyssa *would* be heard. She anchored herself in the middle of the confrontation. "He was only protecting me. You can't arrest him."

"I can and I will."

Determined, she crossed her arms. These men would damn well know she meant business. "I won't let you."

"Oh? Is that a threat?"

"Elyssa." There was a rough edge in Bran's voice. And like any headstrong girl who'd been wronged, she disregarded him.

"Quite possibly."

"For such a pretty little tart, you don't know your place. One more word from you and I'll have you arrested for interfering."

"You crowing, pompous poppycock." Uh-oh. What had she done? Her father would be disappointed to hear her disrespect a man of authority. Or any man, for that matter. So be it. She had enough of being treated like a paltry trifle. She would be a man again and take responsibility for her actions. And *then* send word to Lord Montgomery to beg for her release from prison.

"Step back *now*, Elyssa." Bran nabbed her arm, nearly causing her to lose her balance, and yanked her behind him.

"Hear me, Flynn. I've got an offer you will find most satisfactory." Bran shot her a warning look to not interfere. One she would heed lest she burst into flames.

"For a complete pardon of the *Sanctum* and a promise to leave Mrs. Montgomery's freedom in tact, I will give you the one thing you've always wanted."

"Oh? What could you possibly have that I would want?"

"My head."

Kipp uncrossed his arms, shocked by his captain's declaration. Mac's mouth fell open. Commodore Christensen let out a heavy sigh and bowed his head. Panic tightened in her chest at the men's reactions. She eased up beside him. "Bran, what are you saying?"

The governor's hearty laugh frightened her. This couldn't be. Bran didn't mean it. Surely this was a diversion for another plan.

"A martyr," Governor Flynn said. "How noble. You can't even die without being gallant."

"I knew you'd never give me a pardon, Flynn. Your hate for me is thick in your blood. And you'd deny the *Sanctum* purely out of spite."

"Capt'n?" Kipp's eyebrows gathered, grappling to understand. "You planned this?"

Bran cut his eyes to his first mate. "'Twas the only way to give you and the boys a chance at a reprieve. The ransom for Mrs. Montgomery was merely false colors to guarantee my real design." He looked down to Elyssa. "That's why when you landed in my lap, I saw an opportunity I couldn't overlook."

She couldn't blame him. He was protecting not himself, but his entire crew. With many lives at stake, she'd be selfish to hold a grudge against Bran. Staring into his sincere eyes was more than she could handle. But Bran caught her chin with his fingertips and tilted her head up.

"You will never know, little one, how very difficult it was to see this through. I never meant to hurt you. You must believe that."

She didn't think it was possible, yet she was more heartbroken than before.

He squared his shoulders, raising to full height, and faced the governor again. "Do we have an accord, Flynn?"

"Oh yes, Blackthorn. To be free of you? We have an accord. You will hang by sunset."

"Understood."

"No!" She latched onto Bran. Her lungs constricted. She couldn't swallow enough air—'twas thick with hysterics and closing in. Her mind clouded in a fog of turmoil. Bran would willingly hang? 'Twas insane. *Insane!* She couldn't lose him now.

Commodore Christensen took Bran by the other arm.

"No. You can't take him!"

"Elyssa."

"No, Bran! No placating me."

"Elyssa, my sweet. I meant every word I said to you up on the hilltop last night. You are a burning star in my dark night. You are worth more to me than all the treasure in the Spanish Main. Please, little one. Take comfort in knowing that I have given you my heart." He swiped at the tears streaming down her face with the pad of his thumb. And leaning a little too much on her, kissed the crown of her head.

Bran righted himself. "Mister Kipp," he said. "'Tis been a pleasure commanding the *Sanctum* with you. A word of advice, my friend. Stay away from those fluttering, squawking Frenchwomen, lest you swallow an anchor and get married."

Kipp chuckled, staring at the ground.

"I have one last order for you." Bran clapped Kipp's shoulder.

"Anything, mate."

"Take Elyssa away. Do what you have to, but take her away."

"No. I won't leave you."

Bran peeled her off, winching from the pain in his effort. Fresh blood seeped from his wound. The pain he suffered was the only reason she allowed Kipp to drag her back. She crumpled into his chest, digging her fingers in tight fists on his vest. Her sobs echoed in the hollowed chambers of her soul. Elyssa was losing Bran. She was losing the man she loved. *No! I won't let him hang.* She had to pull herself together, to stop crying. She had to *do* something. *Oh God, give me strength!*

"Shut that girl up, labberneck." Flynn could have swallowed a fly by the looks of his disgusted frown. He rolled his eyes and mumbled. "If I wanted all this mawkish yammering, I'd go have tea with my wife."

Bran nodded he was ready to Christensen. He took two steps and stumbled. Christensen caught him before his knees hit the sand. A lump lodged in Elyssa's throat. She reached for him, but Kipp held her fast.

Flynn cursed. "You!" he pointed to Mac. "Fetch ahead for your ship's surgeon. Bring him to the courthouse. I don't want Blackthorn to die before I can kill him."

"I like your thinking, lass." Kipp retrieved another bottle of rum from a trunk in the corner of Bran's quarters and sat down across from her.

The cabin smelled of the captain, a titillating scent of brine and musk. She had grown to adore his spice while nuzzling into his neck as he made her scream—right where Kipp sat. Heat flushed her cheeks. Thankfully, Kipp didn't notice.

"Blackthorn would be proud of ya. But we've little time to gather the brethren for a rebellion."

Kipp was right. Even if they could round up enough men, they didn't have a plan well executed. *Execute.* A tremor of despair shook through her.

The metal tankard cooled Elyssa's palms. She stared at what was left of the amber liquor. 'Twas her second cup. She swallowed the rest in one quick gulp.

"B'sides, an uprising would revoke any pardon given, Mrs. Montgomery. His sacrifice would be for naught."

Mac knocked and stuck his head through the door. "May I enter?"

"Yes, of course," Kipp said. "Tell what's chanced the captain. What does our man Stumps have to say?" He retrieved an extra cup, filled it, and handed it to Mac.

"Stumps said the capt'n lost some blood. He's just needin' ta rest and he'll live. At least till his neck snaps."

Elyssa winced.

"'Pologies, Miss Elysen." Mac sheepishly looked to the floorboards and drank his rum. Wiping his mouth on his sleeve, he frowned. "The commodore said somethin' strange to me 'fore sending me on my way. Said tarried responses yields enemy gains. What do you suppose he meant by that?"

Kipp shook his head. "Don't know, mate."

"I'm guessin' he means we're runnin' out of time," Mac said.

"Maybe." Kipp scratched his blonde whiskered chin. "Might mean Commodore Christensen meant he'd *give* us time. Aw blast it, I don't know if I trust 'im." He groaned. "Blackthorn does. But I ain't convinced. He's a pirate's enemy."

To Elyssa, it sounded as if they were giving up. "Are you men going to just let him die?" Didn't pirates have a code against letting their captain hang?

"Blazes, no." The corner of Kipp's lip coiled up. "We gotta try to do this right."

Mister Kipp was a cunning man, not given to rash judgments. Elyssa saw why he was Bran's second-in-command. She would take his lead and find another way to free Bran. Maybe with some careful planning…

"I could talk with Lord Montgomery's officer. Surely he could help."

"But would he?" Kipp retorted. "Can't imagine he'd want to want to cast his lot with a horde of pirates."

"He might feel threatened," Mac added.

An idea niggled in the back of her mind. She wasn't sure what it was or even if it was possible. Giddy excitement bubbled forth.

She glanced up at Kipp. "What if you and I use a little persuasion?" she said.

A glint sparked in his eyes. He was on to something, too. "Lass, you are as sly as any pirate worth his salt." He leaned forward in his chair, his gaze sliding between them. "You go on and talk to this officer. Leave the rest to us.

We'll get the capt'n his freedom. With a few grenades and fire-balls, we'll get his freedom."

"Thank you for seeing me, Mr. Sterling." Elyssa took the seat the elderly man proffered. The office was modest in size but not in the material of the furnishings. Dark wood bookcases as tall as the ceiling lined the walls. Scroll work and pineapples were carved into the arms of cushioned chairs. A gilded frame of Lord Samuel Montgomery hung from the wall along with other pictures of important-looking men.

"Yes, well, I certainly have a few questions for you, young lady." He sat behind his massive desk. "Tell me your name again?"

"Elyssa Calhoun Montgomery."

He puckered his wrinkled mouth, nodded, and turned his attention to signing documents on his desk. "As Lord Montgomery's trusted agent of the Bahamas, it is not uncommon for whores and beggars to come knocking at my door claiming lineage or some other ridiculous lie."

He looked down his aquiline nose over the rim of his glasses to scrutinize. The pendulum of a tall eight-day clock clicked, ticking off her courage with each swing. She squirmed under his inspection. This man would be hard to convince the building was on fire, even as the flames licked up his chair.

"A terrible nuisance, I'm sure. But I speak the truth, Mr. Sterling. I *am* the widow of the late Samuel Dobbin Montgomery, daughter-in-law to Lord Samuel Montgomery." She fished out the enamel portrait miniature of Dobie from the pocket of her skirt and slid it across the desk. "I'm not asking for money and you may thoroughly question my authenticity. You may have me jailed if you suspect I'm a fraud. But my relationship with Lord Montgomery is not why I'm here."

"Ah, yes, this emergency." Mr. Sterling studied the round portrait, focusing in, back, and in again over his glasses. "Governor Flynn and his hanging of a pirate."

"Not just any pirate. Captain Blackthorn was once an esteemed officer of the Royal Navy."

Bushy gray eyebrows rose, smoothing out the crow's feet of aged years. "Captain Blackthorn, you say."

"So you've heard of him. Then you know he is admired by men on both sides of the law. You must understand, sir. If Captain Blackthorn is hung, peace and trade for New Providence will be compromised. Pirates will swarm the island."

"'Tis not my affair." He tucked Dobie's portrait into his vest pocket.

"Forgive me, sir, but it will be your affair when Lord Montgomery feels the decline in Nassau's profits and colonists leave for America or Cuba."

The chair creaked under Mr. Sterling's weight as he leaned back, his elbows on the arms and his interlaced fingers resting on his portly stomach. Elyssa hadn't convinced him yet. She mustn't become too desperate. She mustn't panic.

"Please, Mr. Sterling. Captain Blackthorn is to hang in less than an hour." She willed herself not to look at the clock, mocking her with incessant clicks and whirs.

An explosion rocked the office. Pictures rattled against the wall. Vibrations reverberated across her nerves. Elyssa followed Mr. Sterling to the stoop. In the harbor, a blaze engulfed a boat, wooden planks and bits of fire rained to the water.

"Pirates are amassing now," she said. "They seek justice."

More smaller explosions clapped. Swirling gray smoke drifted to the sky in pockets around town. Mr. Sterling was visibly shaken now. His jowls flopped as he swallowed, smacked, and frowned. If she were to admit it, Elyssa felt the rush of fear, too. 'Twas good she was on the pirates' side. She hoped any she met in the building melee knew it.

"Perhaps you could persuade Governor Flynn to halt the execution and avert a catastrophe. At the very least, insist Captain Blackthorn receives a fair trial."

"What is your involvement in this?" He pinned her with suspicion. "If you are not after money, why do you care what happens to this captain or to this port?"

Startled, Elyssa hadn't prepared herself for such a question. Suddenly it seemed everything hinged on her answer. The fate of the world, her world, was on her shoulders. Mister Kipp and Mac depended on her. She couldn't fail. What could she do but tell the truth?

"He's a good man, Mr. Sterling. He hangs so that other good men are pardoned."

Criminy. The longer he studied her, the smaller she felt.

"Very well, Miss *Calhoun*." Mr. Sterling reached for his hat and cane. "Let us go to the square and see Governor Flynn."

Another percussion boomed in the distance.

"Rot me. That better be a raid," Blackthorn muttered aloud. He hoped Kipp was not behind the commotion. Yet, he knew well enough his friend was.

Shouts carried in from outside. A faint but distinctive odor of spent black powder and burning wood wafted in through the crevices of the mud brick stones. *Christ.* Blackthorn pounded his fist on the wall of his courthouse cell. The boys would never get that pardon.

"I admire you."

Blackthorn turned to his visitor. Christensen shoved a key in the lock and opened his door. Two soldiers kept their respectable distance behind Christensen.

"Admire a man who's about to hang by gallows and gibbet?" He patted Christensen's shoulder. "You gone and hit your head, did you?"

"Not many would willingly sacrifice themselves to save another."

"Ah, but you did, when you slipped me the key to escape my last liaison with death."

"No, there was no sacrifice, only risk. And I did so with none the wiser. You…you are intrepid, unselfish, and honorable. Damn it, Bran. What were you thinking? You know some of those men pardoned will go back to the fighting man way."

"'Tis true. I won't deny that. But it is the opportunity I give them to start afresh that matters. Many of them found their way into the pirate trade due to circumstance. Not all are scoundrels." He paused. "They're not much different from you, with wives and children. I won't let them die because of Flynn's hate for me. 'Tis my burden and I alone will suffer the umbrage."

Blackthorn held out his wrists to be shackled. Christensen groused and clamped on the iron cuffs. They weighed heavily. Much like the realization he would soon be dead.

"That is where you are wrong," Christensen said. "You are not alone."

"The men will be fine. And as flattering as you are," he chuckled, "you've got Annabelle."

"I speak of the girl." Christensen leveled his stare. "I saw the fear in your eyes when your man told you she'd been abducted. You've never been afraid of anything, Bran. I saw love and pain, too, when you sent her away."

Elyssa's kicking and screaming as Kipp carted her away skewered him through and through. Her tears had seared gaping holes into his core. He hated himself for the pain he had caused her. Hated that he tainted the angel with his designs.

"She'll find peace and happiness. You'll see to that, won't you, my friend?"

Christensen nodded, offering him a sad smile. "I'll make sure Flynn stands by his decree."

Gunfire popped nearby. The soldiers tensed, readying for action should Blackthorn attack. They needn't worry. Blackthorn had no intention of thwarting the gallows. Not with so many lives at stake.

"Let's get this execution under way," he said. "Before more necks are fitted for the noose."

Warm westerly winds feathered across Blackthorn's face as he exited the courthouse, winds which rushed in under the dying afternoon. The sky, though still bright, had bronzed with the sun's trek to the distant horizon. He scanned the square. Soldiers had strengthened both in the plaza and at various points leading down to the docks. Beyond, in the harbor, several ships had dropped anchor, well within cannon shot. He hoped Elyssa was in a safe place. Trouble was sure to break loose.

Flynn joined them on the porch. "Damnation! Where's that gunfire coming from?"

"Men are fanning out, Governor," Christensen answered. "We're isolating the incidents."

"Well, string him up," he waved a dismissive finger at Blackthorn, "and get this port under control, Commodore."

Blackthorn's one great regret in his miserable life—not beating the shit out of Flynn. Better yet, not killing him. Nay. That wasn't entirely true. He had another great regret, hurting Elyssa.

He marched ahead of the two soldiers, their bayonets at his back, to the gallows. The gibbet's skeletal arm reached out, dangling a hempen rope, beckoning with its hand of death for Blackthorn to come closer. A few onlookers braved the pockets of ensuing chaos of the port attacks and gathered around the platform. They wore curious expressions and none in the faceless crowd hurled the angry curses usually reserved for his ilk. One filthy lad, perhaps a dockworker, stopped Blackthorn. A tense moment passed. Christensen poised to strike down the man, but the fellow stared directly at Blackthorn and handed him a tarnished flask. Grateful for the offering, Blackthorn accepted the bottle. The shackles biting his wrists clanked as he took a swig. The liquor burned a trail to his gut. 'Twas nothing sweeter than to meet his maker with the taste of rum on his breath. He thanked the fellow and continued on to the gibbet where the executioner and priest waited. A priest...how absurdly redundant.

The executioner slipped the rope over his neck and tightened the noose. His skin prickled under the scratchy rope.

"I understand why you did this, Bran," Christensen said. "But I fear Annabelle will never forgive you."

"You take care of that sweet woman, Robert. Tell her I will be at peace." *In hell.*

Christensen smiled that pitiful smile again and stepped aside for the priest. Blackthorn tuned out the man reciting worthless prayers and mercy. He stared across the square at Flynn. The bastard's grin was much too large for his mug. Blackthorn returned a smirk of his own. Flynn's smile faltered. Even in his final moments, Blackthorn rankled his half-brother.

Closing his eyes, he conjured up images of a chestnut-haired beauty with radiant tawny eyes. An angel on his mind was a good way to die.

CHAPTER 10

"Stop!"

Fuck! What is she doing here? Blackthorn craned his neck in his uncomfortable collar. Elyssa parted the crowd, making her way to Flynn. Where was Kipp? By thunder, one order, *one goddamned order*, and Kipp bungled it.

A dapper, hoary fellow managed to keep up with Elyssa. "Governor Flynn," he said, mounting the steps. "I must speak to you regarding this execution."

"Ah, Mr. Sterling, worry none. Pirate Captain Blackthorn will be justly hung in moments. Nassau will be rid of this scourge that for years has vexed our trade."

"There is no justice hanging a man simply because he is what you are not. Magnanimous," Elyssa said.

"What in the name of George is she doing?" Blackthorn said to Christensen. "And who is that old fellow she's with?"

"Lord Samuel Montgomery's officer." Christensen shook his head. "I thought your boys were going to keep her clear from here." He pointed to a group of soldiers, and motioned them to the government house.

Blackthorn could throttle her for interfering. Where the devil was Kipp? Kipp, Mac, somebody, *anybody* needed to get her away from the square, before she got herself imprisoned.

Flynn stared stoned-faced at Elyssa. "Were you aware, Mr. Sterling, that this girl was to be presented to you as a ransom by Blackthorn? I pause to wonder if she was a willing participant in the scheme."

"Ain't true." Kipp, leaning on the government house wall and twirling his dagger in his fingers, edged around the corner of the porch. "The lass knew nothin' of the ransom Capt'n Blackthorn devised for the King's Pardon Flynn denied us. Seems Flynn ain't so trustworthy and Capt'n needed insurance."

"Get this rabble off my porch," Flynn ordered.

Christensen halted the soldiers with a raised hand.

Kipp ignored Flynn and continued. "Even willin' to give his life."

Sterling, stiff as the dead and just as pale, listened patiently, his hands resting on the silver knob of his cane.

Kipp shoved off the wall. "But the boys and I—"

"Belay!" Blackthorn would not allow Kipp to implicate himself in the attacks. "I don't deny the evils I've done. I accept my crimes and I'm ready to die." He lowered his voice for Christensen. "Spare as many of my men as you can and, please, make sure Elyssa is safe." Without waiting for a reply, Blackthorn addressed the headsman. "Whenever you are ready, mate."

Blackthorn chanced one last look at his angel wringing the folds of her dress. Dusk sunlight seemed to absorb into the blue gown, creating a deep vibrant color. 'Twas almost as if Eylssa glowed. A halo of tresses and blue ribbons caught on the sea breeze. Her glistening tears were like celestial stars. There would be nothing more beautiful where he was going and he would savor the moment.

Gunfire split the tension, closer this time. A small explosion, likely a grenado, erupted in a nearby alley.

Screams of "fire" quickly followed. Several men with buckets raced out of the plaza to douse flames.

Flynn took two steps down. "On with it!"

"No." Mr. Sterling spoke loud and clear, silencing the growing anxiety of the crowd. "I advise you, Governor, to halt this hanging."

Only Flynn was more surprised than Blackthorn by Sterling's recommendation.

Flynn took the stairs back to the porch. "You would, would you?"

Flynn stood nose to nose with Sterling. Blackthorn was impressed by the old man. Sterling met the governor's sneer undaunted, lifting his chin a fraction to look at Flynn through his spectacles. The man was as intimidating as a hungry bull shark.

"It is my job to protect Lord Montgomery's investment."

"And I am Governor in Chief," Flynn retorted. "I know what is best for the colony and what is best is to eradicate menaces such as Captain Blackthorn."

"I don't believe a man with the valor and dignity this man possesses is a menace, trading his life for the King's Pardon you are obligated to give under King George's proclamation. You risk an unnecessary war with the pirates."

"Won't be no risk," Kipp piped in, sheathing his dagger. "It'll be certain and swift, it would."

By brimstone, Kipp better know what he's doing. Elyssa is too close in harm's way.

"Commodore," Sterling called. "Won't you set the captain free?"

"No!" Flynn's finger was as pointed as his eyes. "You will do no such thing. Blackthorn will hang."

"Commodore." Sterling tapped his cane on the porch.

Christensen nodded to the headsman to remove the noose. Constriction on his weasand loosened and Blackthorn could swallow again.

"Looks like you cheated death again, brother." Christensen unlocked the shackles from Blackthorn's wrists. He rubbed feeling back into them and rounded his shoulders to relieve his cramped muscles.

"The devil's going to be exceedingly disappointed," Blackthorn said.

Elyssa's look of relief was immeasurable. Blackthorn wanted to go to her, hug her tight, land kisses over her luscious body, and smack her bottom for defying him. But he couldn't. The danger was far from over.

"This is outrageous!" Flynn bellowed. "You've no authority, Sterling."

"Perhaps. But I will remind you that as a confidante to Lord Montgomery, I can request your removal as Governor in Chief."

Flynn ruffled up like a cock challenged for his hens.

"That makes you fairly powerless, Governor," Elyssa said.

Bloody Christ, what was the lass up to now? Blackthorn wished she'd stay out of the strife.

"With respect, Mr. Sterling, mayhap you should consider the request regardless. Surely, New Providence will need a real man to govern. Maybe even a man with the brass of a pirate. 'Twould make the colony safe for trade."

"Why, you little bitch," Flynn spat.

Blackthorn hopped off the gallows platform. That bastard was not going to talk to his woman that way.

Flynn reacted to Blackthorn's approach. He snatched Kipp's dagger from his waistband and nabbed Elyssa.

"Blast! Not again!"

Blackthorn might have laughed by her swearing had the situation not been so dire. He shoved people aside and took the stairs by twos. Flynn shoved Elyssa aside and seized a soldier's sword.

"Bran!" Christensen, running in his wake, tossed Blackthorn his sword.

Metal clashed against metal. An intoxicating sound to Blackthorn. Contact of the swords vibrated in his hand. Aggression pumped in his veins, hostility coursed through his blood like venom. It had been a long time since he fought, truly fought an enemy. Already, he was enjoying the battle far too much. And they had just begun.

Blackthorn parried each thrust and let Flynn lead the fight. Up and down the steps Flynn led them. Once back on the landing, Blackthorn thrust low in quick succession, forcing Flynn to parry low and driving the governor back, back, back, until they had left the porch and were in the rose garden. His wound throbbed from his burst of exertion; the warm ache blossomed up and across his torso. He gritted his teeth to ignore the sprouting pain.

Behind him, the footfalls of their audience bustled on the wooden floorboards. A feminine gasp reminded Blackthorn he had something to live for. The game had changed and he would do everything in his power to hold Elyssa again.

He swung wide, knowing Flynn would duck, just so his blade would lop off the top of a perfectly shaped rose bush. Fresh, floral fragrance filled the air. Red petals and bits of green leaves showered down.

"Oh, bother," Blackthorn said. "Your precious roses."

"You bastard. I'll carve your heart out for that."

Blackthorn laughed. "You may well try."

Flynn roared and charged. Blackthorn spun aside, hopping up onto a square fountain. Blood red roses flourishing from a stone basket sat atop a pedestal in the middle of the fountain. With his boot, he shoved the vessel off the pedestal. Water spattered from the fountain with the impact, and the basket and plant broke apart.

For a moment, Blackthorn thought Flynn's head might explode. Arrows afire with rage shot from his eyes. Cords of anger manifested along his reddened neck.

Blackthorn almost lost his balance off the fountain's edge blocking Flynn's attack.

Blackthorn jumped down. The battle increased in brunt, fueled by fury. Damn how Blackthorn loved a good fight. But he grew weary. The gash in his side no longer ached, it burned anew. 'Twouldn't be much longer and Flynn would have the advantage. Blackthorn needed to end this.

He locked blades with Flynn. Cross guards butted against each other. Their arms shook under the tension. Flynn's rotten breath was as rapid as his own. Blackthorn witnessed the hate Flynn had for him deep in the black cesspools of his eyes.

"This is where we take our leave, *brother*," he said. "Let's make quick of it."

"Flog you," Flynn retorted.

Blackthorn shoved Flynn back and swung his blade. The metal resounded on impact and scraped along the edges as he spun the blades not once, but twice. The quick action twisted Flynn's wrist, disarming him, and the momentum caused him to stumble backwards. The governor slipped on the wet cobblestones. A crack resounded as his head smacked against the ground. A mass of white curls flopped into a puddle.

Blackthorn poked the tip of his sword to Flynn's chest. "I believe you owe Mrs. Montgomery an apology for your slanderous tongue, Governor." When he didn't speak fast enough, Blackthorn pressed harder.

"My apologies, Mrs. Montgomery." Acid dripped from his words.

"I don't believe you meant it." How easy it would be to puncture his flesh and impale his bitter heart. 'Twas too bad Blackthorn's own heart hadn't completely rotted through, or he would have already snubbed Flynn's life. "Again…with sincerity."

"'Tis not an apology I want to hear." Elyssa hastened to the fountain. Her blue gown swished with the lively sway of her hips. Kipp, Christensen, and Mr. Sterling followed. Not one of them resisted stealing a glance at her backside. Blackthorn didn't blame them.

"I want to hear you decree Captain Blackthorn and his entire crew a pardon," she said.

Kipp crouched down beside the Flynn. "Ah, don't look so angry. Ya got a choice, ain't ya? Pardon or die."

"Governor Flynn," Christensen said. "A reprieve would end this contention."

"Traitor." Flynn's nostrils flared, his jaw jutting out in defiance.

"Nay, Governor. I only gave the man a fighting chance. Blackthorn may even be able to help remove pirate activity in the Bahamians waters."

Flynn chuckled. "I'd rather die than have his help."

"So be it." Blackthorn wrapped both hands around the sword's hilt.

Could he kill him? Aye, he could. But doing so would do nothing but satisfy the itch. He, and likely, his men, would face execution. Again. This time, with Elyssa reaching out but not daring to touch his arm, Blackthorn doubted himself. Was there a chance to carry on a life with her? He'd find out momentarily.

Ever so slightly, he raised the sword and leaned in to deliver Flynn's death.

"Wait!" Flynn screamed out, his hands up. "Wait! All right. You win. I'll draw up and sign a pardon for you and your men."

Elyssa squealed in delight, and turned to hug the stiff, and quite startled, Mr. Sterling.

Blackthorn handed the sword back to Christensen and took Flynn by the hand to help him to his feet. Flynn, his lips curled in disgust, snatched up his wig.

"You have my thanks," Blackthorn said, reaching for some modicum of civility. 'Twould be what their father expected from his sons.

The governor straightened his clothing. "Yes, well, there is the matter of the attack on Nassau."

Kipp grinned. "Ain't nothin' destroyed but a jolly boat, fishin' crates, and spent gunpowder. 'Twas the lass's idea. Ya know, just in case you finally saw things our way and give the pardon. If not, ha, that's when the real fun would've begun."

"Elyssa's idea, huh?" Blackthorn pulled her into a hug. Her smile reached her bright eyes. That little armful kept surprising him. By the crinkle of Sterling's brow, she'd confounded him as well.

"Never you mind," Flynn said. "The intent and will was still there and I could have you all imprisoned."

"But you shall not," Sterling said. "You will sign these pardons as your final act as Governor in Chief. I advise you to resign immediately. Otherwise I will request your removal to Lord Montgomery."

A crazed glaze cemented in Flynn's dark pupils, red splotches stippled up his neck, across his cheeks. "You may recommend and request the sea part from here to Montgomery's privy, but I'll not step from my commission."

"Know when you are beat, Flynn," Blackthorn said. "Walk away while your name upon the islander tongue is still relatively untarnished."

"Shut up, you bastard."

"This behavior, Governor, is unacceptable. You have resorted to," Sterling circled his cane in the air, "unprincipled practices. Captain Blackthorn has shown more impunity and righteousness than you. One might say there is a role reversal between you. It's quite shameful—you the derelict and he the dignitary."

"While you're recommendin'," Kipp elbowed Sterling, "the Capt'n, he's a mighty fine leader. He could take ol' Flynn's place as gov'ner."

Not for all the English gold.

Sterling nodded, as if considering such a ludicrous idea. That was the moment something snapped behind Flynn's visage. Blackthorn recognized the look. Flynn's bastioned animosity had crumbled, and he had bloodshed on his mind.

"You have jockeyed what is mine from me—decoration, gold, position, Father's respect—for the last time. Now it is my turn to take from you." Flynn snatched up the sword at his feet and charged toward Elyssa.

No time to think, less time to react, Blackthorn shoved Elyssa behind him, shielding her with his body. The blade, deadly and thin, aimed at his chest. Elyssa's scream echoed in the courtyard. Blackthorn steeled himself, ready, again, to face the unknown that was death.

The blur of metal passed before him. Flynn went down, falling to his knees. An expression of shock froze upon his face. Blood shed from the gaping cleft across his torso on his pristine cream-colored vest. Mouth agape, Flynn toppled forward, landing in the scattered debris of his rose bush.

Christensen, hands gripping the hilt of his grisly, crimson sword, cursed. "Damned fool."

Elyssa peeked up from Bran's shoulder. "Is...is it over?"

"Yes, sweetling. It's over."

Elyssa threw herself into his arms. He held her tight, letting her warmth seep into him. Breathing in the floral fragrance of her hair. Delighting in her rounded breasts pressed against him.

"Oh, Bran. Tell me it's truly over—this whole nightmare. Please. Tell me it's over. I cannot bear not being with you. Not again. I love you, Bran."

Two months ago, he would have shunned such a silly sentiment. Argued love was nothing more than a wistful chit with silly dreams of taming a pirate captain. Never would he share the same emotion, same passion. That was before a rogueling boarded the *Sanctum* and somehow made spoils of his heart. "My precious angel. I love you, too."

Blackthorn held her tighter than he should. But this time he would not let her go. Ever.

The sea could swallow Elyssa whole and she would die happy, with no regrets. Captain Blackthorn made good on his promise. He had reclaimed his bed—with her in it. He had made glorious love to her. Magnificent, glorious love. The flickering candlelight glistening upon wet skin, every caught breath, the sensual aroma of intimacy, lay seared upon her soul. Bran had harmonized carnal groping with tender caresses, his commanding mouth with feathered kisses, and raspy growls with brandied murmurs of her name. She shattered into oblivion with him time and again. And yet, his whispers of love were what she cherished most.

She could have stayed entangled in naked flesh with him forever. Two days had not been long enough. Not nearly.

But he'd asked her to redress his wound as he had business to attend to and must go on shore. He'd been gone for hours now, and she had finally risen from his bed to dress. Elyssa had just resolved to go on deck for a bit of sunshine when Bran returned.

"My angel." He swooped her into his arms, spun her around, bent her low, and kissed her full on.

Dizzy, she giggled. "Mayhap you should close the door, lest one of your men catch you acting buffle-headed."

"Nay." He kicked the door shut. "They'd be envious I have such a bonny lass to hang with from the boughs." Bran kissed her again and set her on her feet. "I have something for you."

Bran loosened a pouch from his sash and placed it into her hand. It weighed heavy and jingled—the sound of coin. Elyssa opened the pouch. The gold inside could light a room.

"What's this?" She didn't understand. Why did he give her gold coins? Verily, she should be paying *him* for passage on the *Sanctum*, though she doubted he planned to collect. Not by way of money, anyhow.

"Your help with my log garnered me a tidy profit." He leaned against his desk, a devilish smirk tilting his mouth.

"Yes, well, this is yours."

He chuckled. "I suppose, in a way, it is. But only because I lay claim to you."

Bran swiped a wayward lock of hair behind her ear. She momentarily closed her eyes and tilted her head into the warmth of his hand. Heavens, but he distracted her so.

"I couldn't."

"You will," he said. "Besides, you'll need it."

That was the truth of it. She was penniless, and she hadn't given regard of what might lay ahead. Bran had stolen any thoughts beyond the next moment with him.

"Sterling has put in a good word with Montgomery for you," he continued.

"Along with the news of his son's death," she said. Her short marriage to Dobie was but a distant memory, yet she could only imagine how the message of his youngest son might affect the Lord Proprietor Montgomery. He may have denied Dobie his whims, but Elyssa knew Samuel loved him. Something occurred to her that hadn't before. "Lord Montgomery might blame me for Dobie's death. I will never gain his favor. Oh, Bran, what if he seeks vengeance on my father and reverses his debt?"

"How could Montgomery blame you for Dobie's insensibilities? Worry none. You'll have your shipping company."

"Please, Bran. Don't ridicule me. 'Tis cruel."

"Elyssa, my love. The only thing I want for you is your happiness. I would never ridicule you for your dreams."

Bran pushed off the desk and grabbed a bottle from a chest. A quick twist and the cork popped out. 'Twas not rum. It had a sweet, heavy aroma.

"I save the Madeira wine for special occasions," he said, handing her a cup. "Let us celebrate the *Sanctum* and her new commission." He raised his cup and took a sip.

"I don't understand."

"My ship, it is small. My crew, they are hardy. 'Tis not much, but both will serve as a start for your venture. And I may not be good at arithmetic, as you spare not one chance to remind me," he winked, "but I happen to have the respect of many merchants in many ports." He wrapped his arm around her waist crushing her into the curvature of his taut body to which she fit so well. "So, you see, you *will* have your company."

The knot of emotions filched her ability to speak. She tried, even moved her mouth. It was all she could do but nod. Nod and focus on his sinful grin.

She had gone from a widowed sailor boy pressed into service on a pirate ship, became a rogue's pawn in a dangerous family feud, and fallen in love with the pirate captain. And now, in an odd twist of fate, she was to become his business partner. Bran had taken care to see to her future. Men usually don't welcome women into their occupational affairs. Yet, Bran wanted to stand by her, to see her reach for her dreams and succeed. How was it possible to love him more? One thing for sure, her adoration for him had no bounds.

"Together, darling, we will prosper—as husband and wife."

Slowly, she set down her wine. *Husband and wife?* Elyssa's vision blurred, a lump lodged in her throat.

"I hope those are tears of joy," he said, dabbing away a teardrop with his thumb. "What do you say, little one? With the blessing of your father and Lord Montgomery, will you be my wife?"

She leapt into his arms, excitably whispering 'yes' between kisses. Elyssa's heart was so full, yet it floated past the glittering stars on the winds of heaven.

"Guess my plundering days are over. I've all the spoils I could ever want right here." Bran laughed, giving her arse a tight squeeze.

"Oh, please say it isn't true." She awarded him a coy smile of her own. "I happen to enjoy it when you go a-rogueing. Most especially when you fly your jack and show no mercy."

"My angel, you wear the devil well."

"I've a pirate to blame." She winked.

"Ah yes, well this pirate also happens to be very good at giving orders."

Bran unraveled her legs from around his waist and set her down. He rounded his desk, pulled out a piece of paper, and dipped his quill in the inkwell. "My first order of business." He handed her the white plume. "A letter home."

She hugged him with such ferocity, he coughed for air. "I love you, Captain Blackthorn."

"And I love you, more than you could ever know. Now sit."

Gladly, she did as he bade. Yes, the sea could swallow her whole. But not just yet. She had a lifetime she wanted to spend with a pirate.

Dear Father,
Please forgive my tardy letter. I am well and, by virtue of an honorable pirate, have an amazing adventure to tell.

About the Author

Jennifer Bray-Weber has always wished for real life to mimic fantastical tales of adventure, especially those of the high seas. Holding two degrees, one in Music and Video Business, the other in Liberal Arts, she continued her higher education, that is, until a professor challenged her to further express her creative talents and write a novel. Never one to back down from a dare, her passion led to writing stories of pirates, with her debut novel *Upon A Moonlit Sea,* since re-titled *Blood And Treasure,* among the 2009 Golden Heart historical finalists.

Though she hopes to one day live out her life as an island goddess somewhere in the Caribbean, Jennifer currently lives in her native state of Texas with her husband and two daughters.

For more information on Jennifer and her upcoming releases, please visit her website at www.jbrayweber.com.